The BIG BLACK DOG

The BIG BLACK DOG

Thomas Elliston Smith

authorHOUSE®

AuthorHouse™
1663 Liberty Drive
Bloomington, IN 47403
www.authorhouse.com
Phone: 1 (800) 839-8640

Published by AuthorHouse 05/07/2018

ISBN: 978-1-5462-4158-4 (sc)
ISBN: 978-1-5462-4156-0 (hc)
ISBN: 978-1-5462-4157-7 (e)

Library of Congress Control Number: 2018905601

Print information available on the last page.

CONTENTS

CHAPTER 1 The Bullies

I SAT ON THE cold, wet ground with my arms wrapped tight around my legs, which were now pulled up so close to my chest that they hurt. I couldn't move just yet, though; I needed to wait a little longer. I knew that if my hunters didn't find me soon, they would leave, and then I could get my books out of the dumpster, where I was sure they had tossed them, and head home. They hadn't bothered me much outside of school, but I knew I'd brought attention to myself at school today when Marvin Sikes and his boys were picking on some new kid. They knocked his books out of his hands. My luck wasn't any better. His books hit me in the back while I stood at my locker. As I turned to complain, I saw the school bully staring at me with those fiery eyes of his. "Oh, look who's getting tough, boys," Marvin said as the first bell rang.

"Saved by the bell, kid, but we'll see you after school," he announced loudly. That's when I knew I was in big trouble and that I had better take the long way home after school.

Marvin Sikes was a seventh grader but looked like he should be well into high school. He was tall and a little overweight. My plan worked well to begin with. As the bell sounded, I gathered up my books and quickly made my way to the bathroom, where I could hide in a stall until the school cleared out. I stood on the seat of the toilet so no one could see my feet. After about ten minutes, all sounds were gone and

I was hoping it was safe to leave. I grabbed my school bag, which was wedged between my legs on top of the seat, and slowly opened the stall door. I stepped down softly and made my way over to the door that led to the hallway. I made my way down the hall, from one classroom doorway to another. As I stood in the last doorway, peeking out to see if anyone was around the main door, I heard a deep voice from behind me. I knew it wasn't Marvin and his boys, but I was startled enough to drop my school bag. I turned to see the school janitor walking up behind me. For a big man wearing those big boots, he sure walked quietly. My first thought was, *I hope he's friendlier then he looks.*

"Good afternoon, son," he said with a smile. "Is something bothering you?"

I stuttered out a "No, sir," as I bent down and picked up my bag.

"Well, if there is and I can help, I surely will, but if not, it's time for me to lock myself in this big building and start to clean, unless you want to stay the night and clean with me. I'm sure I can find things for you to do."

"No thank you, sir. I think my mom and dad will be waiting at home for me."

He laughed at that and said, "I'm sure they will. You have a good night, and by the way, most people call me Big Mike. And you?"

I was on my way out the door as Big Mike spoke, but my mind was on my hunters. Big Mike held the door open as I stepped outside to look around. Having found the coast to be clear, I answered him with, "My name is Paul."

"Okay, Paul, I'll see you again."

"Yes, sir," I said.

I made my way down the street, going away from my house. I thought two blocks would be far enough. I turned into an alley that I had used once before to get away from these guys. At ten years old in a city as big as Chicago, I was afraid of everything, but I couldn't let them know that or else they would call me a sissy and pick on me more. I sure didn't like these alleys, but I had no choice. I made my way down about a block, past the backyards, garages, and garbage cans of all the houses, thinking I was safe. But to my surprise, there they were, only fifty feet away. All five of them were standing in front of me, just like statues. They all wore big, heavy black boots and had long silver chains hanging from the thick, black leather belts that held up their dirty blue jeans.

I turned slowly but kept my eyes on them. At first they didn't move, and then I saw Marvin smile at me and say something under his breath. They came running, yelling like they were madmen. I took off running as fast as I could. I was a fifth grader, and I could run pretty fast, but not fast enough. My knees were weak, and I was covered in a cold sweat. The thought of these guys beating me up made my heart pound like a drum. The sweat reminded me of blood running down my body. These guys were seventh graders, and even with those heavy boots, they caught up to me before I could make it to the end of the alley. Marvin didn't run after me; he let his boys do his dirty work. I thought for sure I was dead, but somehow I turned and swung my book bag with both hands locked together on the handle and hit the first guy, Jake, who was almost as big as Marvin. I got him good in the chest, and he went down, grabbing at his chest and yelling some foul words in pain.

The guy right behind him reached for me, but I stopped. Now I'm not sure if it was out of fear or if I just wanted to give up and get this over with, but as I stopped, I stepped to the side to duck a punch Barry threw at me as he ran past me. I threw my school bag at him and got him in on the leg. He went down, too, on one knee, and I heard something inside me yelling, *Run, run!* And I did just that. I took off past him. I bent down to grab my bag while in a full run, but I missed. I didn't have to look back; I knew the others were right on my tail. A burst of energy mixed with all that fear kept me running just like the racecars with a special fuel I had seen not long ago at the racetrack with my dad and Uncle Bud.

Down the alley to the street, I took a quick left, running as fast as my legs would carry me. This time I knew for sure that if they caught me, I really would be dead. I ran down two blocks to the next alley, where I stopped and hid behind the corner of a building just long enough to catch my breath and to peek out to see if they were after me. There they were, only now they were walking. Marvin was in the lead. He had my book bag tucked under one arm, laughing and hitting

Barry, the guy behind him, on top of the head with his free hand. Jake, the guy I had hit with my book bag, was following far behind, still holding his chest.

I turned and ran down the alley. I found a place behind a dumpster to hide. I slid in behind it and covered up with some wet paper and cardboard. It wasn't long before I heard their voices coming down the alley. I was sure they were going to find me and beat me up with those chains, just to watch me bleed. But as they got closer, I heard Marvin telling the others that they were a bunch of sissies for letting me get away and saying that he was going home. I heard a dumpster not far from where I was open and slam shut. I was sure that was my book bag being tossed. I didn't think they would take my books home with them; I didn't think any of them could read. I wanted to laugh out loud at that, but I caught myself, not knowing if they were still around.

I waited a few minutes before pulling myself out of my cave. I poked my head out slowly to find a pair of eyes looking down at me from across the alley. I gasped for air, in fear of death. I thought for sure it was Marvin and the boys. But after my eyes got used to the light, I saw an older man, tall and thin, with gray hair, a thin gray mustache, a very white shirt, and a black tie tucked into a long white apron. "Young man! What are you doing playing in that garbage?"

"Well, sir! You see ..." I stuttered out an answer, not wanting anyone to know I was running from school bullies, just like I had with Big Mike at school. "I was looking for boxes because we may move soon."

"Okay," he said. "Looking for boxes, huh? I guess that's a good reason for crawling around in rat-infested garbage. But what's wrong with those boxes piled up over there? I know they're clean; I put them out this morning. Now tell me a story I can believe! Was it those big boys I saw a few moments ago? Bullies?" he asked.

My eyes opened wide with surprise, but I said nothing. I was speechless. How did he know? He said nothing more while I pulled myself free from my hiding place and stood to brush myself off.

"Are you okay, my young friend? I mean, any blood or anything? Or is that just dirt and garbage on your hands?"

"I'm fine, sir," I said, turning my hands over slowly to see an ugly, stinky mess staring up at me.

"Come in the store and wash your hands and clean that mess off your pants."

"No, thank you, sir. I'm already late getting home."

"Well, I think it's better to go home a little later, clean, than have to explain where the dirt came from, don't you?" he asked. "Besides, I'm sure you won't like telling that bully story."

"Well, I guess you're right. I'll be right back," I said. I made my way over to the closest dumpster. I tried to open the lid, but it was too high for me. I stood looking around for something to stand on.

"Are you looking for a school bag, my friend?"

"Well, yes, sir, I am. How did you know that?"

"Well, those boys are always around here looking for trouble, or something to steal, so whenever I hear them, I look out the back door and they take off. I think you'll find your bag in that big red one over there. Get that five-gallon paint can over there and stand on it. I'll help you open the dumpster."

We opened just one side of it, to find a real mess. "Oh boy, they sure don't like you!" the man said.

"No, sir, and I really don't know why."

"Well, son. By the way—what is your name?"

"My name is Paul, sir. And yours, sir?"

"Well, you can call me Mario."

"Okay, Mario."

"Well, Paul, as I started to say, bullies don't need a reason to pick on people. They just like to act tough because they're not. Also you'll find that bullies aren't very smart, and that's why they run in a bunch. You don't see them picking on people who will fight back. They're just like these rats out here in this alley. I think we should get your bag and clean you up so you can get home. In addition, here's where things stand right now. Paul, you have two choices: one, climb in and get the bag, and you'll be a bigger mess, mainly because that Chinese restaurant doesn't bag their garbage—I think they sell it as pig slop—and two, you go clean up and I'll put a nail in a board and we'll fish out your bag when you're done."

In the store, Mario gave me a towel and pointed me in the direction of the bathroom. It didn't take me long to finish, but Mario had already fished my bag out of the garbage and cleaned it up. "I think it will take a few days for the smell to go away," he said.

Before I left, he showed me around the store and gave me his phone number. "If your mom and dad have any questions, have them call me." As I was leaving the store, I stopped to thank him. I said, "I'll be back again, sir, if that's all right with you."

"That will be my pleasure, Paul."

"Thanks, and maybe I'll bring my mom and dad in someday too."

"I'm looking forward to that," Mario said. "And, Paul, watch out for your school chums."

"I always have to do that, Mario," I said as I left the store.

Well, moms will be moms, and mine sure was mad at me for coming home from school forty-five minutes late. She was even more angry at me for getting my clothes as dirty as they were. "You smell like you were rolling around in the garbage, Paul." I wonder what gave her that idea? "What were you doing, Paul, to wind up smelling like you do?" she asked in a very harsh voice.

"I was playing a game with some of my good friends from school, Mom. I think you call it hide-and-seek."

"Well, don't do it in the alley anymore. And go change your clothes. I'll need to wash them now—or should I say burn them?" She gave me that mom look. I thought it best not to say another word as I left the room. Mario was right: I really didn't want to tell that bully story to anyone ... ever!

CHAPTER

2

Jail Time

I WOKE UP FAST the next morning to my dad's voice calling me from the hallway. "Paul!"

"Yes, Dad?"

"Speed it up a little. Today I'm dropping you off at school."

"Okay, Dad."

This was unusual. Mom always dropped me off on her way to work. I wondered if they knew what had happened yesterday after school. Maybe Mario had called them. But I didn't think so. He didn't have my number. Maybe Big Mike had told someone at school, and they called. If that was it, I really was dead.

I ate my breakfast while Dad was on the phone. Once he had hung up, he said, "Let's go, Paul. I need to get you to school. I have a meeting. We're already running late."

"I'm ready, Dad."

On the way to school, I said nothing. I just sat and held my book bag in my lap, staring down at it, hoping my dad wouldn't ask about the smell. I was sure my life at this school was over for being a squealer, even though I'd told nobody. Mario had only guessed because he knew Marvin and his boys were troublemakers.

"Dad?"

"Yes, Son?"

"Where is Mom this morning?"

"She had to be at work early today."

"Oh. And you're going in late?"

"Yeah. I'm the boss. I can do that sometimes." He looked at me for a response. I just nodded my head. I said no more. I just sat hunched over a bit, playing with the straps on my bag.

I knew Mom would be at school to meet us. That's why she'd gone in to work early, so she could take off for a short time today to make this meeting about the bullies with Dad. I'd have to go see Mario about those boxes again, I needed them now. I wondered how much I could carry once I ran away from home. I almost laughed out loud but caught myself.

As we pulled up in front of school, my dad said, "Paul, are you all right?"

"Yes, Dad. Why?"

"You're awful quiet today. Usually you're yelling out the window at your friends a block away."

"Oh, I'm a little tired, Dad," I said, as I looked around for my mom to come running up to the car.

"Oh, okay!" Dad said. "Then here you are, another day of learning for you, and another day of being the boss for me." He reached across the seat to hug me, but I didn't move at first.

Then it all hit me: no Mom and no Dad meant no school meeting. I gave him a big hug back and said, "Thanks, Dad. I think I just woke up."

"Son, sometimes I think you're a strange little boy. You might need help." He pointed at his head. We both laughed and waved goodbye.

As I walked up the front stairs of school, it hit me again. I shouldn't be happy! I was going to get beat up real bad. A fifth grader had hurt the bullies and then got away. Oh boy, was I in trouble. If I would have thought of it, I would have asked my dad if we could move to the country tomorrow. Well, it was too late now; I was surely going to get beaten up after school today.

As weak-kneed as I was, I made it into school on my own, with my friends pushing and shoving, wanting to be the first to tell me the news.

Their voices were half drowned out by my fear. I knew Marvin and the boys were around somewhere, hiding, just waiting to trip me, pants me in a crowd, or merely bop me on the head a few times, just to get me ready for the big beating after school. I looked around, but I didn't' see any of the bullies.

"Are you listening to me, Paul?"

"What did you say, Jerry?"

"I'm trying to tell you over all this noise, no more school bullies." Jerry was my best friend. We started school together and somehow we'd just stayed together ever since. He was a little loud and made himself heard, and as my mom said, he was always in fast motion.

"What are you talking about?" I asked.

"They were here early this morning," Jerry said, "sitting outside waiting for school to start."

Yeah! Or waiting for me, I thought to myself. "Yeah! Yeah! Go on!" I said.

"Well, the police came and took Marvin and his boys off to the jailhouse, but nobody knows why yet."

"In a police car?" I asked.

"No, in two police cars," Jerry said. "With the lights flashing and all."

"No kidding?" I said.

"Marvin and the rest went quietly," Jerry said, "but Jake gave the cops some trouble and they almost beat him up. He wound up on the ground. The cops handcuffed him and carried him to the cop car and almost threw him in it."

"Wouldn't you know it?" I said. "The only day I'm running late, something good happens."

The first bell sounded, signaling that it was time for us to go to class. Everybody scattered except—yep!—me. My thoughts went wild again. Could this whole thing be because of me? Oh boy! I wanted to tell my parents as soon as I saw them, but I thought it best not to. My mom would worry too much, and Dad would take it too lightly and make a joke about it. Then Mom would get mad at him and me.

The next three days went well at school, but on Friday, as I entered my first-period classroom, I saw a tall skinny kid who almost made my stomach turn. Barry was Marvin's whipping post. He was one of the boys. In fact, he was the one I had hit in the leg in the alley. Sometimes I thought he was more afraid of Marvin than I was. I was sure that if he was here, the others would be close. But to my surprise they were nowhere around.

Barry didn't say a word to me. He just walked out when the class ended. That whole day I worried about what after school would be like. Well, I soon found out.

It was Friday! My last class of the day was gym. As I headed over to the locker room, I heard Jerry calling my name from his last-period classroom. "What?" I said.

"Meet me out here after school. Don't leave until you talk to me."

The late bell rang, so I yelled an "okay" and made it into the locker room just before the gym teacher. He yelled a not so friendly, "Let's go, gents. Time's a-wasting."

After school the halls were filled with people trying to get in and out of their lockers, just the same as I was. However, I took a moment to think about how nice it was at this school without Marvin Sikes and the other four troublemakers. I heard Jerry's voice from down the hall, but he was shorter than me, so it was a while before I saw his head pop up in front of me. "Paul! Paul!" he yelled as he grabbed both of my arms. "You have to come outside and hear what I've got to tell you."

"Okay! Okay!" I said.

"Did you see Barry today?" Jerry asked.

"Just in my first class, but he was very quiet."

"Well, he had a lot to say later to us."

"Tell me now!" I yelled.

"No! Not here."

Outside was quiet now; most of the kids were gone. "Okay!" I said. "Now tell me."

We sat down on the front steps. "Well, Marvin and the boys, Barry told us, were out together till late Monday after school."

"Tell me something I don't know," I said under my breath.

"What?" Jerry said.

"Nothing," I said. "Go on."

"Well, they headed over to the train yard to steal some food and soda from the workers' lunchroom. Barry said he was with them once before when they did it. But before they got there this time, they started shooting rocks at that new office building, on Webster Avenue, with their new slingshots they had just stolen from a store a few minutes before, and knocked out a bunch of windows, until one of the guys hit the main window in front of the building. Barry said that must have been the only one hooked to the alarm at the time because it was a new building. The alarm went off, Barry said, like a fire siren stuck in your ears, and they took off and ran till they couldn't run anymore."

"Is that why they went to jail?" I asked.

"No. Listen to this. After they rested, they wanted food more than ever. They got up to go. They were walking under that el train by Webster Avenue, and Barry's dad drove by and saw them. He made Barry get in the car and took him home. When the cops came to school, they arrested all of them because they know they all hang together."

"But not for the windows?" I asked. "Then what?"

"Well, it seems the other four of them got to the train yard and waited for it to clear. Then they went in and took some food and drinks, and then they broke into a toolshed and stole a bunch of the workers' tools. They got away, but two people saw them leave and called the cops. The cops arrested them all at school here, but they had to let Barry go because he was home with his mom and dad at the time of the incident. Barry said they're all going to be home for a few days and then be back at school."

"Oh, aren't we lucky?" I said.

"Maybe they'll be better," Jerry said.

"Do you think so?" I asked Jerry. "And would you bet your life on that?"

"No," he said, "but we can hope."

"See you, Jerry. I've got to get home, and your mom is waiting."

"Do you want a ride home, Paul?"

"No thanks," I said. "I like walking when there's no wild animals to attack me, like the bully boys."

Holding My Breath

CHAPTER 3

"PAUL, ARE YOU READY to go yet? Your dad is waiting in the car."

"Yes, Mom, I'll be right down."

"Okay, let's go," she said.

"Why do I have to go to the hardware store with you and Dad?"

"Because you're too young to stay home alone all day, and we have other stops to make. We may be gone too long."

"Mom, I'm going to be eleven years old soon."

"Yes, Paul. And I let you stay home a lot when I go out for a short time and I'll be by a phone, but not all day. That's too long to be alone."

Saturdays are great, until we have to go shopping, I thought to myself. But I knew it wouldn't help to argue, because around our house Mom was the boss.

"Good morning, Paul," my dad said with his usual smile as I got in the car. My answer was not chipper, and he made a joke about it. "You sound like a tiger this morning," he said.

Mom told him, "He's mad at the world today because he has to go shopping with us."

"It's a nice day," he said, "and we'll have a great time." My dad was a funny guy. He never really got mad about much.

"First, I think breakfast will be great. I'm starving," he said. Not far from our house was the pancake house, one of my favorites. I guessed the day was getting better already, although I didn't want to admit it to Mom.

As we walked into the restaurant, the first person I saw was Jerry, sitting with his parents. He jumped up and ran to me as if he hadn't seen me in a year. "Slow down," I said as I grabbed him, before he could knock us both down. "Paul! You won't believe who's home."

"Do I get more than one guess?"

"Yeah! Sure," Jerry said.

"Marvin and the boys, right?"

"Yeah, right! But how did you know? They just got home this morning."

"They're the only ones I know who were gone."

"Yeah! Well, I guess," Jerry said. "But what you don't know is that they are really mad at you for something you did last week to them."

No! That was Monday, but who's keeping track? I said to myself. "Where did you hear that?" I asked.

"Well, I only live one block from Jake's house, and his sister and mine run around together. His sister Mary tried to find out what made them so mad at you, but Jake wouldn't tell her. The only thing he would say was you had better leave town fast. She said he is a nutcase and so are those guys he hangs around with, and now that they were in that detention center and have to go to court next month, they're worse than ever."

"Look, Jerry, please don't say a word around my mom and dad about this."

"What are you going to do? They'll hurt you if they get the chance."

"Well, I'll try not to give them that chance if I can help it. But telling will just make it worse." I hadn't told anyone, not even Jerry, about the book bag into Jake's chest.

I heard Jerry say under his breath, "Here comes your mom with that fire in her eyes."

"Are you boys eating with us or what?" my mom demanded as she walked up behind me.

"Oh, sure, Mom, I'm starved."

"Yeah! Me too." Jerry said as we headed off to our tables with my mom leading the way, looking pretty mean, and with Jerry and I looking at each other through the corners of our eyes and making our own scary faces.

Well, that news sure ruined my day, and maybe the rest of my life. I know for sure it ruined my breakfast. I was sure Dad found something wrong with my appetite too, but all he said was, "Not too hungry, Son?" I didn't answer; I just started to eat a little more. Dad knew that Mom didn't like me leaving a lot of food when we went out to eat. He also knew she would get mad if she saw that I did. So while she was talking to Jerry's parents, Dad reached across the table and took two of my pancakes with his fingers. Jerry saw him eat them in just a few bites. With his mouth stuffed, we all looked at each other and laughed. Dad almost lost his food all over me. Mom was none the wiser.

We said our goodbyes and left the pancake house. Then we headed over to a small hardware store, where Dad said he needed to pick up some new locks for the doors on our house. He told Mom and me that the neighborhood was getting worse and he wasn't taking any chances. *You're telling me about the neighborhood,* I said to myself, without cracking a smile.

To my surprise, the store we were going to was right across from Mario's deli. I let out a yell that scared my mom and dad half to death. "Paul, have you gone nuts?" my mother asked.

"I'm sorry, Mom, but I know the man who owns that deli across the street."

"You mean Mario?" Mom asked.

"Yes, Mom. Do you know him?"

"Of course, Paul," she said with a stern voice, "that's where we buy all that lunch meat, cheese, and bread we use at home and for the parties we have at home and at work."

"Dad! Can I go over there and say hello while you and Mom are in the hardware store? He's a really nice man."

"Maybe I'll go with Paul," Mom said. "And, honey, you can come and get us when you're done. I'll place an order for his man to deliver Monday."

"Good idea," Dad said. "I'll be awhile. Be careful crossing that street. And don't forget the cannoli," he yelled. "He's got the best in town."

Now I'm not sure if this is a good idea or not, I thought to myself. *What if Mario says something to Mom about the bullies and me?* "Mom, are you sure you don't want to stay with Dad and help him pick out locks for the house? I can cross the street by myself."

"I'm sure you can, but I know nothing about locks, Paul, and I'd rather buy food than locks."

Well, I guess I'll have to hold my breath until we leave, I thought. *I'm in enough trouble at school now, without Mom over there yelling and calling the cops because of something Mario says.*

Meet Black Dog

CHAPTER 4

WHEN WE WALKED IN, Mario turned to look out at the door as the bell rang. He saw Mom first, and greeted her. "Good morning, Mrs. Collins."

Mom replied with, "Mario, how are you today? I think you know my son, Paul?"

His eyes lit up a bit as he stretched to see over the meat counter. "Oh yes, we met one day not long ago when"—that's when my heart dropped—"he was out back looking for boxes and we talked. I gave him a lecture on how bad alley rats could be."

Oh! Thank you, Mario, I thought. I looked up at him to see him smile slightly. I had to smile back at that rat story.

"I had no idea, though, that he was your son," Mario said. "However, now that I know, I can see the resemblance to his dad. By the way, how is Daddy Paul doing?"

"Oh, he's fine. He's coming over after he buys some new locks for the house. He's across the street."

"Oh, that's good. I want to tell him, and you of course, what a nice son you have."

"Well, thank you, Mario."

"Can I get you something today, Mrs. Collins?"

"Yes, I want to place an order for Monday's delivery. After five, please."

"Great, but I need a minute, if you don't mind?" Mario said. "I have some things outside the back door I need to move or else they might walk away. I'm sure you know what I mean?"

"I do, Mario," Mom said. "That's why Paul is across the street buying new locks for the house. He said the neighborhood is changing. I'll look around and make a list for your deliveryman."

"Excuse me then," Mario said. "Paul, you want to help an old man move some boxes? You look pretty strong."

"Sure," I said.

"Paul, can you grab that bucket of old meat? I just cleaned out my deli and I need to toss it in the dumpster. You know what a dumpster is, right, Paul?" He laughed out loud.

I set the bucket down just inside the back door. I looked at him with a stern face and turned to see if my mom could hear. Then I said very quickly, "That's not funny, Mario," as I gave him a look that could kill. Then we both broke out in a laugh. We moved all the boxes into the store. Mario told me to close the door, saying that he was going back to help my mom. As I reached out to swing the door closed, I thought I really was going nuts like my dad had said a few days ago. I gasped for air and couldn't breathe. As sure as I lived, I saw a gigantic black bear standing on all fours, looking right at me. When I finally caught my breath, I swung the heavy steel door closed hard. I stopped it before it slammed, but it still knocked me into the store. After I had taken a moment to think about whether or not to open the door again, I took a good grip on the door handle and leaned into it. Slowly I pushed the door open again, but only enough to peek out. I saw nothing. Slowly I pushed it farther and farther, until I could see most of the alley. At first, I thought I was crazy. There were no bears in Chicago, unless maybe one had escaped from the Lincoln Park Zoo. But, oh my Lord, there it was, the biggest animal I had ever seen up close in my life that wasn't in a cage. It was as black as coal and sure looked mean.

My mom and dad had always told me not to mess with any animals I didn't know, but there was something about this one that drew me to it. Then I remembered that bucket of meat Mario had me carry to the back door. It was still sitting inside. I peeked into the front to see what Mario and my mom were doing up there. Mom was talking and writing, and Mario was just taking it easy, leaning on the deli counter. I moved quickly to the back door and reached into the bucket. I grabbed a chunk of meat and tossed it over to where I'd last seen the huge animal. But the creature was gone. I took one step outside the door, holding onto the door handle so that if the animal were to attack me, I could slam the door. But it really was gone.

I went back to peak up front one more time. My dad wasn't there yet, so I went back out the door slowly to see if the animal was around. I wish I knew what this thing was, because then I wouldn't have to call it "it." I slowly made my way down the alley past the chunk of meat I'd tossed out. I passed the rear doors of a couple of stores, being careful not to make any noise. I didn't want to scare the creature away again. "It sure looked like a big black bear," I said to myself, "so I'll at least call him Bear."

I decided to head back to Mario's, but as I turned to do that, I found Bear blocking my retreat. Oh my Lord, he was bigger than I had thought, standing there with his head held high. He had a head as big as a bear's, with a set of eyes as dark as the piece of coal he looked like, and a tail that wrapped up and over the rear part of his back. He was beautiful and stood proud as he blocked my retreat. His ears pointed straight up. I knew now this could not be anything other than some type of great dog. My heart was pounding and my sweat started to flow, but I didn't dare move my hand to wipe it away, for fear of making Bear mad.

I slowly slid my fingers partway down into my pockets so Bear couldn't see them shaking. I was more afraid of this animal than I'd been of anything ever before in my life, including the bullies. I didn't know what to do next, but I was sure mad at myself for getting into this mess. But how lucky I was at the same time that it wasn't a bear. I was afraid to look at him, afraid he might get mad and attack me.

I sure had to go to the bathroom, but I couldn't move. *Mom and Dad must be buying out the stores they're in. They don't even know I'm missing. And what about Mario? Where is he? Maybe he's paying too much attention to my mom and has forgotten all about me. Maybe he doesn't know I'm in this rat-infested alley, as he calls it.* I closed my eyes for a second, and when I reopened them, I found the creature lying on the ground, eating the meat I had tossed out.

Then all of a sudden it hit me: he's eating that meat I tossed out. I had passed it by as I walked this way looking for him. He had to have come up from behind me. Now he was lying there as if he didn't have a care in this world, and I was scared to death and ready to wet my pants. If he wanted me, he could have had me then. *Well, enough of this! I am going to stand up to him. Then again, maybe I should go out this way, around the front of the buildings, to the front of Mario's store. No, that's not a good idea. What if he chases me, like the bullies did? It was only this past Monday when I had to hide from them right here in this same alley. Boy oh boy, I really have to go to the bathroom. Okay, this is it! I'm walking right past him. That's it, here goes.* But my feet wouldn't move. As I stood stiff, thinking of what to do next, I closed my eyes again for just a second, to imagine how great it would be to be in the bathroom, and to wish the animal would just take that meat and leave me alone. But this time when I reopened my eyes, he was gone. He had taken the meat and hadn't even made a sound. I looked down the alley to see if he was anywhere around, but it was like he had read my mind. He and the meat were gone. Then something hit me again: *Oh boy, do I have to pee!*

I guess I didn't care anymore, because my feet started to move before I'd even thought about it. I wasted no time getting back to the store. As I entered the rear door, I almost ran head-on into Mom. She was trying to tell me that they were wondering where I was. *Well, maybe you should have come looking for me,* I thought as I ran by her. "Sorry, Mom, I need the bathroom real bad."

Come to find out, Dad was out front and they were ready to leave. I really wanted to stay at Mario's and had to think of something fast. I knew my mom wanted to drag me with her and Dad through all the stores, but I wanted to stay at Mario's. I needed to talk to him about that animal, which by this time I was sure was some kind of dog that I had never seen before.

Well, it didn't take long to get a no from Mom and Dad. Mario said, "Stop by anytime after school, if it's okay with your mom and dad." We said our goodbyes and headed out to our next stop.

CHAPTER 5

The Bullies' Big Surprise

LIFE HAD COMPLETELY TURNED for the worse. It all started Monday, back at school. Marvin and his boys were on the hunt again. They took no time letting me know I was the hunted, making their comments and swinging at me as if they wanted to punch my head in. Marvin still had Barry at his side most of the time. He wasn't allowed to be seen with Jake, Sammy, and the smallest but meanest of all, Little Hank. Barry never said anything to me while he was with Marvin; he only tried to look tough. The boys couldn't do anything bad in school, Jerry told me, or else they'd have to go back to the detention center and stay there until it was time for them go to court next month. "You couldn't prove that by me," I told Jerry.

I walked out of my classroom, on my way to lunch, and Barry grabbed me by my arm. I pulled away before I knew who it was. He was a seventh grader, twelve years old, and a lot taller than me. "Listen," he said, "I'm here to help you, but I haven't got a lot of time. If Marvin or the rest of them see me talking to you, I'm dead. We are all getting together to find you after school today. I don't want to, but I don't know how to get out of it. Be extra careful not to run into Jake. He's real mad about you making him look bad in front of Marvin and the rest of us. I've got to go." He yelled that last bit as he turned and bolted away. Then he stopped and yelled, "Hey, Paul! Good trick with that book bag." He gave me a small grin, reached down, tapped at his leg, and disappeared into the crowd.

I wanted to smile back, but I realized I had nothing to smile about. I was in big trouble, and even if Barry wanted to be good, the others wouldn't let him. The first thing I needed to do was to get home safe today, and then I would think about what to do next. I was sure it was dumb not to tell someone about the bullies, but I knew my life would be over if I did.

The bell rang to end the day. My heart was racing. Again I gathered up my books and made my way through the crowd to the bathroom, but this time I needed to go. I opened the door to find Jake using the urinal. I turned and ran after he'd looked right at me. The hall was still filled with enough people for me to disappear into the crowd. I didn't bother to look back; I just wanted to get out and run. My heart was pounding and again I felt weak-kneed. I headed for the front door as fast as I could walk. I sure didn't want the other kids to know I was running away from Marvin and the boys, but somehow I knew they were all watching me.

I got to the front door and stopped just inside it to look out, to find Marvin and Barry standing at the top of the stairs, acting like big shots. At the bottom of the stairs stood Sammy and Hank. I backed up into the hall, and turned right into Jake. "Going home, squealer?" he said.

"Yes," I told him, "and I didn't squeal."

"Well, maybe not, but you did hit me with that bag, and I owe you for that."

"What was I supposed to do, stand there and let you guys beat my head in?"

"You better run home every day, because we'll be looking for you. Today you get a pass, but never again." Jake turned and walked outside, down the stairs, and past Marvin and Barry without saying a word. I wondered why they were giving me a pass today and only today. Maybe Mario was right. Maybe because I'd fought back they wouldn't bother me again, but then again, maybe Jake's sister was right and they did want to hurt me real bad. Well, I didn't think I wanted to take that chance right now. I looked for Jerry to get a ride home with him, his sister, and his mom, but they were gone.

I thought it best this time to stay out of the alley, out where there were people. Jerry told me these guys couldn't be seen together, so maybe they wouldn't bother me on a busy street. I headed out the back door of the school, went down one block, and turned right. Other kids were taking the same way home. I had to put up with some heckling, but it was better than having to confront Marvin and the boys.

About halfway home it got real quiet and I was more alone then I wanted to be. Other than a few cars on the street and an old bearded Oriental man walking the other way across the street with a long wooden cane, I was alone now. I started to walk a little faster. I didn't get far before I heard voices saying, "Squealer. Squealer."

I looked around, but I couldn't see anyone. All I could hear now was the sound of the old man's wooden cane as it hit the concrete in the distance. I knew I should run, but which way? I knew Marvin and his boys wouldn't let me get away again. Maybe it was time to tell someone about them. Or maybe it was too late. I felt tears starting to build up in my eyes. I knew crying wouldn't help, but I couldn't help it. My heart was pounding in my ears like a drum. I knew they wanted to hurt me, and I was alone and scared. I knew I had let it go too long this time.

Again I heard the voices: "Squealer, squealer, squealer." Then I saw Jake and Hank standing up ahead of me, with their silver chains hanging from their belts and their heavy black boots on, which I knew they were going to stomp me into the ground with. These twelve-year-old kids now looked older, bigger, and meaner than they ever had before. I turned to run, but this time I had to face Marvin and Barry, walking toward me from the other direction. Then from a gangway between two buildings right next to me, Sammy appeared. He lunged out at me, grabbed my arm, and took my book bag away from me. Marvin started laughing.

"Oh, look, boys, he has no weapons now to beat you sissies up with." Marvin grabbed me by my shirt as Jake and Hank walked up behind me. He picked me up, spun me around, and threw me on the ground. By now I was so scared that the tears started to roll faster. "Oh, look, guys, he's crying. Hey, Jake! You can have him first; you owe him bigtime. Then you can have him, Barry, for hitting you in the leg with that bag. Then if he can walk, maybe we'll let him go home. But if you tell anyone we did this, squealer, next time it'll be worse—and there will be a next time." Jake had a smile on his face as he reached down and pulled me up. "I'm going to hurt you real bad!" Then he stopped talking. The smile melted off his face like hot wax. His eyes opened wide and his lower jaw dropped as if he were at the dentist office. He was staring at something in the same gangway that Sammy had come out of. My back was to the gangway as he held me, so I couldn't see what was so startling to make him quit talking.

Then I saw Marvin's eyes open wide. He said quietly, "Jake! Let the kid go." Jake still held me tight, but Marvin yelled once more, "Let him go now!"

Jake said, "Yeah, I think you're right."

"Hey, kid," Marvin said softly, "is that thing yours?"

"What thing?" I asked, tears still built up in my eyes.

"Turn around, Paul," Marvin said. They all stood like statues as I turned slowly to see the most wonderful sight I had ever seen in my lifetime. The big black dog that I had seen in the alley in back of Mario's store stood facing us, only this time he didn't stand proud with his head up and his tail bowed over his back. He stood leaning forward with his head down and his tail pulled under him. He looked meaner than any black bear.

But Jake, as with the police at school, wanted to prove he was tough. He grabbed me by the back of my shirt, pulled me backward, and yelled, "I'm not afraid of some dumb dog!" As the words came from his month, the black dog lunged from the end of the gangway across the sidewalk and onto the grass, where Jake held me by the back of my shirt. Black Dog stood facing Jake, with his beady black eyes burning a hole in Jake's body and his teeth shining like silver razor blades from everywhere in his mouth. A very strange sound was coming from deep down inside him.

Marvin said very softly, "Jake! That dog weighs more than you and me put together, and if that dog goes crazy out here on us, I promise, you will be my first victim when we get out of the hospital—if we get out of the hospital."

"Okay, Paul!" Jake said, letting go of me. "But it's not over yet." Then he reached out and pushed me away, but he pulled his hand back quickly as Black Dog snapped at him. Jake fell backward to the ground. Black Dog hovered over him for a moment with one very large paw on his chest and growled with his face just two inches from Jake's nose.

I yelled, "No!" and Black Dog backed off. We all stood in silence.

Marvin said, "Paul, we weren't going to hurt you! We were just trying to scare you. That's how we have fun, that's all.

"Now tell me this, Paul," Marvin said, "is that your dog?"

I thought for a moment, and said, "Yeah! I guess so."

"Well, let me ask you something else, Paul."

"Yeah, what's that, Marvin?" I asked, wiping away my tears with both hands.

"Can we leave now, or is he as mad as he looks?"

"Well, Marvin, let's say you'll have to find that out for yourself, because, you see, guys, I haven't had him long enough to know. But one thing I do know: whatever you do, do it very slowly."

"Yeah! I think you're right," Marvin said. He turned slowly and put out his hand to help Jake up. Then he started to walk away with his boys right on his tail. Thinking about my book bag that Sammy still had in his hand, I started to say something, but Black Dog now sounded out louder and meaner than before, with a growl that made all of us shiver, as if again he had read my mind.

Marvin turned quickly with a look of fear in his eyes and became as white as a ghost upon seeing Black Dog ready to do battle again. "I thought you said we could leave."

"You can, but I think you'll have to leave my book bag."

"Give it back to Paul," Marvin said to Sammy with a harsh, mean voice. Slowly Sammy handed me the bag. I looked at Black Dog. The sound was gone, but he still stood as though he wanted to eat those boys. They all stood as still as possible, looking from Black Dog to me. I wanted to laugh, but I thought, *Well, after all, I'm not sure of this dog much more than they are.* I nodded my head at the boys, but they hesitated. Then they turned slowly again. My head followed them just to be sure they left. I had to laugh at the way they were walking so slowly. They put one foot in front of the other and all walked in a straight line as though they were walking a tightrope, until they were out of sight. I turned to thank Black Dog, but again he was gone. I walked down the gangway he'd come from, but he had disappeared, even though the backyard was completely fenced at least seven feet high and the gate to the alley was locked.

CHAPTER 6

The Search Is On

Back home with all my body parts in order, I helped Mom get dinner ready and straighten up the house, because Grandma and Grandpa were coming for dinner. "Paul," Mom said, "why are you being so helpful?"

"I just thought you needed help."

"Well, I appreciate it, but normally you don't help unless I beg or pay you."

"No reason, Mom." If she only knew. I thought this would be a good time to ask for my own dog, while Grandma and Grandpa were here. They would back me up. My dad always had a dog when he was growing up, even though I was sure it was nothing like the one I wanted to bring home.

As dinner ended, I thought this was a good time to pop the question. I knew the answer already, but I had to ask. I wasn't sure how to ask, so I just blurted it out in front of everyone. "Can I have a dog?" I said. The house sure got quiet. All eyes shifted right to me. Not a word was spoken. My dad looked around at Mom, and then he looked at my grandparents. I wasn't sure why, but Grandpa had the biggest smile on his face as he looked at my dad. Somehow, even at almost eleven years old, I knew my dad had asked the same question of his dad some years back.

Mom was the first to answer. "Paul! We have had this talk before, and you know the answer."

"But, Mom," I said, "back then you said I was too young and I wouldn't be able to take care of a dog. But now I'm almost eleven and I can and will take care of it."

"It's just too hard to have a dog in the city, Paul," Mom said.

"But Gram and Gramps have always had a dog and they live in the city."

My dad and grandparents sat quiet while Mom and I did all the talking. Their heads bobbed just like those little dolls you win at Riverview with the wire in the neck, from one of us to the other. "You have to teach a dog a lot of things," she said, "to make it a good city dog."

"I will, Mom. I promise."

"Paul," my dad said, "if you got a dog, would you be willing to feed and water it every day before school and do everything it needs to live right?"

"Yes, sir," I said, as I leaped from my chair, "I sure would."

"Well then, if you can make your mom believe that, you have my vote."

I looked at Mom and saw the look she was giving my dad. "You men always stick together," she said. "Well, I guess a dog it is." She smiled. "But Paul, this place has a small backyard, which must be kept clean. And no two-hundred-pounders like Dad and I heard you dreaming about the last few nights."

My eyes opened as wide as they could go. I couldn't believe they hadn't told me about the dreams before this. But I was going to get my dog, and that was all I wanted.

"We can start working on finding a dog this weekend," Mom said.

Dad yelled out, "I can take him to the pound Saturday!"

"No way," Mom said, "am I letting you two go without me. You'll wind up with that dream dog of Paul's." Dad and I started to protest, but Mom cut us short. She held up a hand, as to say she was finished talking. She made her point. "No me, no dog," Mom said. Dad and I just sighed. Gram and Grandpa just looked at me and smiled. "By the way Paul, did this dog thing have anything to do with you being so helpful today?"

"No, Mom. Why do you ask?" I smiled at her.

"Yeah! Just as I thought," Mom said, "just like your father."

My next problem wasn't as easy to deal with. You guessed it, the boys. They sure let me know they weren't finished with me, but for today I didn't have to worry, because I was going to the library after school with Jerry and his sister, and his mom was driving me home after.

Patty made her way into the library while Jerry stopped me at the door. "What is so important that we have to get today at the library and that you can't get at the school library tomorrow?" Jerry asked.

"Well, remember when I told you that Marvin and his boys were hunting me after school? I didn't tell you any more than that because I didn't want anyone in school to know I've been running from the bullies. Now I have something to tell you. You won't believe it. I'm not even sure I believe it yet." We stood outside the library until I finished telling my whole story to Jerry. This was the first time since I'd met Jerry that he listened to anything without interrupting twenty times. "Jerry! I need you to help me find all we can on this kind of dog."

"But I've never seen it," he said. "How will I know what it looks like?"

"You'll know when you see it, from what I describe to you."

"Okay!

"Oh, Paul, tell me, how did you get my sister to come down here?" Jerry asked. "I don't remember her ever going to a library. I didn't even think she knew how to read."

I just shook my head. Patty was Jerry's older sister by two years, but their relationship was what made me happy I didn't have a sister. "Well, I heard her talking to her friends, and she said she loves cannoli. I told her I could get the best cannoli in town if she could help me out, and here we are."

"Wow! Paul, you're good." Patty stuck her head out the door and asked us if we were coming in.

"Yeah!" Jerry said.

"Okay, let's get to work," she said.

We spent the next hour and a half looking through every dog book we could find.

Just before closing time, Patty found us knee-deep in books. "Did you guys find what you were looking for?"

"Well, we found some look-alikes, but it's not the one I'm looking for. What about you?" Jerry said to Patty.

"No! Me neither. I wouldn't have believed there were so many books on dogs. In ten more minutes we'll have to go," Patty said. "It's closing time. Did you ask the librarian for help?"

"Yeah! She told us if we didn't have a name, we should start going through the dog books."

"We better get these books put away or we'll get fed to the dogs," Patty said. "The janitor is waiting to start his work, and those are not friendly smiles he's showing on his face."

We put the books away and started to leave. We almost made it to the door. "Are these your books here?" the janitor said. Patty and I both looked at the cluttered table across the room and then at Jerry.

"That's where you were working," Patty said to Jerry. We cleaned up and put the books back on the shelf while the janitor looked on. Then he reached across the table and picked up one of the remaining books. That dead face of his seemed to come alive. "You have dog questions?" he asked.

"Yes, sir," I said.

"Well, maybe I can help."

"You know dogs, sir?"

"More than most, I guess. You see, I used to work as a dog handler, at the dog shows all around the country. That is, until I got sick and just couldn't take the moving around from state to state and running with the dogs anymore. Tell me, young man, what are your questions?"

"Well, sir, I'm looking for a very large black dog that looks like a bear, and when he's mad his head hangs down and his tail curls under. His eyes are coal black and rather small and close together. His teeth shine like silver razors."

"Oh boy," the janitor said, "that's a great description. Do you sit at home dreaming about this dog?"

"Well, my mom and dad said I do." Everybody laughed at that.

"I'm sure you do," he said with a smile. "But that sure sounds like more than one dog I know. Tell me, son, does this dog that you hunt have a good side too?"

"Well, yes, sir, he does," I said. The others looked at me. "He sometime stands like a statue with his tail wrapped up and over his back and with his head held high." "Sounds like a show dog to me," the janitor said. "Well, one more thing: Have you ever been able to touch this animal?"

"No, sir, I was too scared he might eat me. He looks like he weights two hundred pounds."

"Well, that's smart, son. Not all dogs are friendly. But as I started to say, the hair on this dog looks a lot like a bear's?"

"Yes sir!"

"Then follow me," he said as he turned away from us. Then we all spun back around to a voice saying good night. It was the librarian, as she left the building. The janitor gave her a short wave and turned back to lead the way. "Have you looked at the old newspapers over here?"

"No, sir, but why would we want to look there?"

"Well, the dog that you hunt may not be listed in many books as of yet and probably hasn't been in many shows in the States. It's 1955, and this dog, if it's the one I'm thinking about, only started showing up somewhere around the mid- to late 1940s out of Japan. And I've only seen one that was all black. I hope this is like the one you're looking for," he said, sorting through some old newspapers. Then he stopped and was silent. He just stared down at the papers. His back was to us, so we couldn't see his face. Jerry, Patty, and I all seemed to be holding our breath at the same time. Then he spun around so fast that he scared the three of us to death. We all jumped backward. He stood facing us with a smile on his face and said, "Kids, I think we hit the jackpot." He held up an old newspaper with a large picture, and a front-page story whose headline read, "July 5—Japanese emperor visits USA." And next to the emperor stood a big black dog just like the one I was searching for.

They all looked at me for reassurance, and that they got. I saw the picture and went numb. When I came to my senses, they were all yelling, "Is that it, Paul?"

"Yes, yes that's him," I said.

"Well, now wait, my friend, I don't think that's the same dog, because this picture was taken in 1945, ten years ago. But after the war some American solders did bring these dogs back from Japan. Some GIs wanted them because they were thought to be good luck for women having babies. And it was believed they could help sick people get well. Others wanted them because they wanted to brag about owning a dog that could track a bear into the cold mountains of Japan, and that's exactly what these dogs were used for, hunting panda and deer. They can withstand temperatures way below freezing because of the two layers of hair they have. The bottom layer is thick and soft and holds in the body heat, while the top layer is rougher, to keep out the cold and wet weather. They have no problem sleeping deep in the snow and blowing cold. It's believed that Helen Keller was the first in the USA to bring this dog back here after it was given to her as a gift by the Japanese government. Sorry, I talk too much when it's something I know, after working alone all night." We just laughed. "This dog breed has come a long way and may be the oldest breed of dog known to man. It's called an Akita. And on that note, I must get to work, and you, my now good friends, must go home to your awaiting families. Any other questions?"

"Sir," I said, "how did you know about that newspaper and the dog?"

"Well, I'll tell you, if it's in this building and has anything to do with dogs, I can find it pretty fast, and you can bet I've read it. That's how I knew about this Akita. And one more thing, there not all black. Any other questions, ask for Randolph. Have a good day and travel safe." We walked out saying goodbye, and he locked the door. I turned to thank him, but like the big black dog, he was gone too.

CHAPTER

7

Find Black Dog

WELL, FOR NOW LIFE was good. Four of the bullies were not at school. Patty told Jerry and me that it was their day to meet with their lawyers. It sounded like they were in big trouble. And Jake's dad was really mad at him. Patty, Jake's sister, said Mary told her that her dad wanted to put Jake in a military school out in Indiana. *Well, as much as I like him, I sure wouldn't miss him,* I thought to myself, but I said nothing.

After school I headed over to Mario's store. Just as I was about to enter, I heard a much too familiar voice, "Paul! Paul! Where are you going?" Jerry was yelling at the top of his voice.

"Where did you come from?" I asked. "I thought your mom picked you up?"

"She did, but she had to make a stop down the street. And while I was sitting in the car, I saw you."

"I have to see Mario," I said. "I have to see what he knows about the black dog."

"I'll go tell my mom where I'm at, and then I'll be right back," he said as he hurried away.

Mario was stacking shelves along with his helper/deliveryman when I walked in. I opened the door slowly so as not to ring the bell too loud. Mario looked up from the floor. A smile spread across his face as he stood to greet me. He asked, "What brings you this way today, Paul?"

"I need to speak to you if you have time."

"I always make time for my friends," he said. Then he said, "George, this is Mrs. Collins's son, Paul."

"We've met," I said, "when he delivered to our house. I just didn't know he worked for you." George answered with a quick "hi" and a shake of his head, and then went back to work.

"Now what's on your mind, Paul?" As I started to talk, the front door of the store slammed open and that same loud voice rang out again. The bell on the door sounded like it was going to explode. Jerry almost fell into George's lap where the latter was working. Jerry came in very hard and fast, but Mario somehow reached out and grabbed him at the last second. "Slow down, my young friend. We have plenty for everyone."

I just shook my head and looked away. Once everything settled down, Mario said, "Go on, Paul."

"Well, Mario, remember when I was here with Mom and you and I moved those boxes inside and you told me to shut the door?"

"Yes, Paul."

"Well, I saw a really big black dog out there."

"Oh! There are always dogs hanging around out there, Paul," Mario said. "We have great garbage, but every once in a while our fearless dog catchers come, remove the dogs they can catch, and take them to the pound."

"Then what do they do with them?" I asked.

"Well, Paul, some that are friendly they clean up and find families for. Mean ones, and I'm sorry to have to tell you this, get put to sleep."

"You mean killed, Mario?"

"Well, yes, Paul. But I hear that at the pound they save a lot more than they put to sleep."

'That's mean, Mario."

"Yes, Paul, it is, but if they let all these dogs out to roam the streets, the dogs would be in big trouble. First, they wouldn't find enough food to live long. And then they would start to eat other animals. And if they eat or even get bit by a sick animal like a rat or another dog, they get sick too! That's were rabies come from. Do you guys know anything about rabies?" I said no. Jerry just shook his head.

"Well, remember this. If you get bitten by a dog, or any other animal for that matter, or even scratched by a cat and it draws blood and gets away, and can't be tested for rabies, you will have to go to the hospital every day for ten days and get a shot in the belly. I know this to be true. My grandson was bitten a few years ago and we couldn't find the dog. He was only eight years old. So now that you know what you know, please stay away from stray animals. That goes for cats too. And the rats in the alley," Mario said, this time without a smile on his face.

"Is there any way to tell if they have rabies?" Jerry asked.

"Yes, sir. Take your animals to the family vet. There are shots for that and other things that can hurt your pet. Keep them home, clean, fed, and watered, and they will love you like you love them. Well, boys, I have to get the store ready for Saturday's rush. Is there anything else, Paul?"

"Just one thing, Mario. Have you ever seen a dog out there that looks like a big black bear?"

"I don't think so, but then when I open the door, I always make enough noise that they just run away. And that's how I like it. Just like the boys run who like to hang out back there smoking and looking for things to steal." Jerry and I laughed and said our goodbyes.

As we left the store, Jerry asked me if I thought maybe that big black dog had been picked up by the dog catcher. "Well, I thought about that too," I said. "Tomorrow my mom and dad are taking me to look for a dog at the pound. I don't want any other dog. But I want to see if he's there."

"Can I go, with you?" Jerry asked.

"Sure. I'll call when I know what time we're leaving. Hey, Jerry! Think your mom will drive me home now?"

"Sure. I think she likes you better than she likes me anyway."

"That's because I'm better-looking," I said.

"Yeah, right!" Jerry said.

CHAPTER

8

The Pound

"REMEMBER, PAUL," MY MOM said as we were getting ready to go to the pound, "no two-hundred-pound dogs—and no one hundred-pounders for that matter."

"I know, Mom, I remember," I said, trying not to use a harsh voice, but I knew by the look she was giving me that I'd gotten caught. She just shook her head and turned away. It was still clear to me that Mom didn't really want a dog. "Where's Dad, Mom?"

"Having his car washed. Then he is coming back to get us. We'll pick up Jerry and go to the pound."

"Oh! I forgot to call Jerry."

"That's okay, he called before nine o'clock this morning, but you were sound asleep. You can call him when your dad comes in and tell him to be ready."

"Mom, we are just going to look, right? I mean, it's up to me what kind of dog I get, right?"

"Yes, sort of," Mom said. "There are rules in life, and you already know the rules. That the dog is not too big is the most important rule. Your dad is here. Let's go." Then I heard her say under her breath, "Saved by the bell," as she let out a big burst of air. "Call Jerry," she said.

After we picked up Jerry, we headed off to the pound. The pound was fuller than I would have ever thought. There were so many dogs and cats without homes. Some were so small that they could fit in my hand. Some were so big that they needed a farm to live on. Jerry took time to look at most of them with my parents, but I rushed through to see if I could find Black Dog. I found nothing that even looked like him. And not one dog caught my eye. I wanted to find him, and I wouldn't settle for anything less.

I found my dad and Jerry looking at the dogs, and Mom was in the cat room with a kitten in her arms. I was sure she was going home with it, but she said she wasn't, and left it there. "Some other time," she said, "after we get settled down with a dog. Did you find the one you want, Paul?"

"Not yet, Mom, but I want to keep looking."

"Okay then, I guess we'll go and then come back another time. They're about to close. They're not open late Saturdays."

We gathered up Dad and Jerry and started to leave, but first I talked to one of the men who worked there, without Mom and Dad around. I described Black Dog. "I have to say, young man, I'd sure remember that dog if I'd ever run into him. But as of this time, I've never seen him. But I'll keep my eyes open."

"Thank you, sir," I said. "My number's in the office. My name's Paul Collins."

My dad was more surprised than anyone that we were not taking home a dog. I just told him I needed more time to think. And not another word was said.

CHAPTER

9

My Mad Dad

SUNDAY WAS ALWAYS GOOD around our house. Jerry was over, as were a few other friends. We played some baseball in the empty lot not far from my house. Our bikes were parked up against the building next to it. There were a lot of our friends around, so we didn't chain up our bikes. When it was time to go, I found that my bike was missing. Someone had taken it while I played ball. But no one else had lost theirs. I stood, looking around, wondering what to tell my parents. As Jerry and some other kids rode around the neighborhood looking for my bike, I headed home to face my parents. They'd always told me to lock up my bike.

When I was almost home, I saw my dad sitting outside with a few neighbors. As he looked at me, I could see his face change from a block away. For a guy who never got mad, he sure wasn't happy. I said nothing as I walked up to the house. The other men just stared, knowing there was something wrong but not sure what. "Where's your bike, Paul?"

"It's gone, Dad. Someone took it." I knew the next question and was sure I didn't want to hear it. I didn't want to tell him I hadn't locked it up.

"Was it locked up, Paul?" That's all it took. I let loose and cried like I'd never cried before. "Now is not the time for tears, Paul," he said as he stood. "Where did it get taken from?" As my dad spoke, Jerry rode up with a few other friends and told us that they couldn't find the bike. Dad said, "I'll take my car and see if I can find it."

One of the neighbors said, "We all know that bike. We'll go in our cars and go this way." He pointed.

"Paul, you go tell your mom what happened and where, and tell her to call the police." I said nothing. I just shook my head and went in the house. Jerry and the other guys left.

It wasn't long before we heard sirens going down the street, but Mom hadn't called the police yet, so we thought Dad had gotten a hold of one. It wasn't long before we heard Jerry pounding on the door and yelling louder than ever. "Paul! Paul!" I swung open the kitchen door. He started by saying, "You won't believe what happened at the park." This time I listened as Jerry talked. "A bunch of kids were playing ball, and they heard some kid screaming at the top of his lungs for God to help him, over and over again. He was being chased by this dog that looked like a bear, big and black. Paul, that sounds like that dog you're looking for! Someone called the police. The kid rode by on the bike, and the dog was right behind him. The kid tried to outrun the dog on the bike, but the dog was too fast and he didn't make it. Some people say it looked like this dog could fly, because he leaped so far through the air. They say the dog took him down, somewhere by the Lincoln Park lagoon. I tried to get close to see if it was your bike, but the police wouldn't let anyone near. I do know that the kid was lying on the ground and the ambulance had just gotten there. The kid telling me the story described your bike right down to those streamers on your handlebars. He said they saw the dog leap through the air and knock the rider off the bike. He said the kid hit the ground pretty hard, and the bike went down the hill and hit the concrete wall at the lagoon."

Mom stood leaning on the counter, as if she needed the support, with her eyes opened wide and her mouth dropped in amazement, just listening to Jerry talk, which was real strange, as she never listened to Jerry.

When she finally spoke, her words were soft and she seemed to stutter a bit. "Did the dog bite the kid?"

"No, Mrs. Collins. At least the kid telling the story didn't think so, but he must have come close, because he had part of the kid's shirt in his mouth as he ran off and out of sight. I couldn't get closer, so I left to come and tell you. On the way here I saw your dad in his car, so I waved him down and told him the story. He told me to tell you that he was going there to find out if that was your bike."

It was awhile before we heard Dad at the front door. He opened the door slowly and closed it gently as he always did. Now with most people you could tell by the way they did things whether they were mad or not. But such was not the case with my dad. The only way to tell if he was mad was to see is face—just like today, when he saw me coming down the block without my bike. I'd seen his face change from a block away, and so had the neighbors. Just one look at his eyes and you knew he was mad.

My dad crossed the living room and walked into the kitchen, where Mom, Jerry, and I stood waiting for him to speak. His first words were, "Paul! We have to talk, but first I want you to listen." Mom started to say something, but Dad held up his hand to stop her. Jerry and I looked at Mom to see how well she would deal with someone doing to her the thing that she often did to us all. Then again, Mom was the boss in our house and she knew it. Her eyes opened wide and her jaw dropped. But this time she said nothing more. As she regained her composure, she nodded at Dad as if to say, *Go ahead.*

Dad began to speak, and again Jerry interrupted him. "I'm sorry Mr. Collins, but I have to go home. I'm already late." Jerry was making his way to the door as he spoke, not waiting for my dad to say a word. As he opened the back door, he said, "Good luck, Paul!" Then he slammed the door and was gone.

Mom and Dad looked at each other, saying nothing until Jerry was out of sight. Then Dad asked without any more hesitation, "Do you know a kid named Barry Lambert?"

"Well, yes!" I said. "Barry goes to my school. Why, Dad?"

"Well, this Barry kid took your bike and crashed into the wall down at the Lincoln Park lagoon."

"How's the kid?" Mom asked.

"He's going to be okay. But he'll need some rest. It seems, Paul, from what he told the police just before they took him away in the ambulance, that you ran into him and a few of his friends after school the other day and that you had this dog with you that looked like a black bear and was just as mean. He said you sicced the dog on them, and that one of his friends was so scared that he started to cry and you made fun of him. He also said that you told them to walk away very slowly or else your dog would have them for lunch."

Oh boy! I thought. *This guy sure knows how to change a story around.* I tried to break in a few times, but Dad would not stop talking. He told me to let him finish and then I could talk. That's when I realized that maybe this was why Mom didn't let him have too much say-so at home. I almost broke into a laugh, but I knew better and caught myself.

Dad said, "This kid told the police that this dog of yours chased him down, flew through the air, and ripped part of his shirt off, knocking him off the bike. The cop said that a few more feet and the kid would have gone right into the lagoon. I told the police that we don't even have a dog. Now, Paul, we have one other thing we'll have to talk about before we're done."

Mom looked bewildered again but said nothing.

"What's going on at school, with these bullies?" Dad asked. My body lost all feeling as I tried to figure this whole thing out. How did Dad know about them, and how much did he know? I needed to answer fast.

"A few big guys at school like to harass the little guys and the new guys," I said, "until they find out if they'll take it or not. All you have to do is stay out of their way, Dad. They're not that tough." I wanted to tell him what Mario had told me about alley rats, but then I thought better of it.

Mom's voice sounded out louder than ever after Dad had said the thing about the bullies. No raised hand was going to stop her now. She jumped to a standing position with her arms both raised high, as though she were looking for help from God, but all the time she was looking at me for an answer as she spoke. "Have these bullies been bothering you, Paul, or picking on you?" she demanded.

"No, Mom, not really," I said quickly. *I sure hope Dad doesn't say any more. If he does, Mom will be out of the house and beating on Barry's door, and there would be no stopping her.*

Dad calmed her down by telling her he'd heard from the police that this kid was new at the school. Speaking to me, he said, "And this Barry kid said he took your bike because you sicced your dog on them. He said he was going to give your bike back at school.

"What is with this dog thing, Paul?" my dad asked. "It sounds like that same dog we heard you dreaming about a while back."

Well, I knew that was coming, but I still had no answer. After all, I wasn't sure if my best friend, Jerry, had believed me about the story of the big black dog, so why would my parents?. I started to tell them the story about Black Dog helping me out of a jam with the boys down that street on my way home, but just then Grandma and Grandpa came through the front door like they were on fire and needed water. They wanted to hear all about the bike and the park and, of course, the police. Dad looked at me and asked if I would have any problems at school with these boys.

Now I'm not sure about anything right now, I thought to myself, *but I am tired.* I just needed to wait and see. I sure didn't want any more talking. "No Dad," I said, "they really don't bother me. Am I going to get my bike back, Dad?"

"Yes! But it's going to need work before you're able to ride it again. And I'm real sure Barry's parents won't like paying for it.

"Paul, if you're sure you're going to be okay at school tomorrow, we'll talk when I get home from work."

"Okay," I said. I knew Dad didn't want to talk in front of Gram and Grandpa; it would just get them upset. I said my good nights and headed up to my room.

The next morning I got a ride to school with Mom as usual. And that's when she told me that Jerry's mom would drive me home. "I don't trust those boys," she said. "Jerry's mom will be taking you home till school is out."

"But, Mom," I said, "I'll be okay."

She said, "You don't know that, Paul. Just a few weeks and school will be over." *Yeah, that's just great!* I said to myself. *Now I'll never see Black Dog again. I might as well be a prisoner.*

School Ends

CHAPTER 10

Well, I knew the thing I needed most today was about the dumbest thing I could want. I needed to talk to Barry. I thought it might have been some other dog that had taken him off my bike. And I wanted to know where this dog had come from, and if it was Black Dog. I knew Barry wasn't in the first class, so I asked around, and found he was still out after that Sunday bike ride in the park. What I found out next I really didn't want to know. The rest of the boys were back in full swing.

Marvin cornered Jerry and me by the bathroom, looking tough and thinking mean thoughts. The only thing wrong with that picture was that Marvin knew Jerry had an older sister who had an older boyfriend, and we all knew Marvin never wanted to see him again. It seemed Marvin and Jake had been at the movies one day causing trouble as usual. Some girl told them to be quiet, Marvin dumped his popcorn on her head, and Jake rubbed it in her hair, and then they ran out of the theater laughing. Well, they didn't laugh long. The girl was Jerry's sister, Patty. Her boyfriend found Marvin and Jake a few days later looking in store windows. He moved them into an alleyway, and with two of his friends he made them unable to go to school for a few days. But on their return, they were told not ever to look at Patty again. I guess that meant they'd better not look at Jerry either. Boy, sometimes I wished I had an older brother, or sister for that matter.

Marvin started to get mean. But I think he knew that he didn't want any witnesses, so he just gave me a dirty look and walked away. The rest of the school day went as best as it could with these bully boys trying to make my life as rough as they could. I hadn't seen Black Dog since my long walk home, and I was pretty sure the boys didn't want to run into him again.

Black Dog was gone, but I sure hoped the dog catchers hadn't gotten him.

So far the bullies had been, as they say, out of sight, out of mind.

My eleventh birthday had passed, and brought me a new bike. Mom and Dad bought it for me, but I heard Grandma telling one of her old, hard-of-hearing friends that Barry's parents had written a check for it. My dad and mom asked me right up until school was out if I'd had any more trouble with the bullies, so I asked them to say "the boys," not "the bullies." I wanted to forget the word *bully* for the rest of my life. They agreed.

I spent most of my time between my house and my grandparents' house, which were only a few blocks apart. Mom didn't like me staying over at Jerry's house. She said he was too loud and his motor never stopped running. I had to beg, but with Dad's help, she gave in. I could stay at Jerry's from Friday night to Sunday. Dad and I couldn't tell her up front about going fishing on Saturday or else she wouldn't have let me go. She was afraid of water and thought I would fall in, even when I was with Dad or Grandpa.

I had to admit, Mom was right about Jerry's motor. It never stopped. We didn't get any sleep Friday night, but we fell sound asleep Saturday morning. It almost wiped out our fishing trip. It was eleven o'clock by the time we left his house. We tied everything onto our bikes and headed out to the lagoon. His mom didn't know that my mom didn't like me fishing, so she packed us a lunch and told us to be careful and have fun.

Everything was going well until I saw Marvin come from the concession stand. Right behind him was Jake. I looked around for the rest of the group, but I didn't see them. Jerry was sitting on the concrete wall with his feet hanging over the water. I called quietly, but he didn't hear. So I walked over and called his name so no one else would hear.

But this was Jerry I was dealing with, and there was nothing quiet about Jerry.

"What, Paul?!" he yelled out. I turned my head away so Marvin wouldn't see me.

"Quiet, Jerry. Marvin is right over there with Jake."

"Where?" Jerry said, as he spun around on the wall to face them.

I said, "Too late. Here they come."

"Oh, look, Jake!" Marvin said. "No dog. What happened to your mutt? Or do you think of him as your big brother?"

"Well, they sure look alike," Jake said.

"That's true," Marvin said. They laughed about having made what they thought was a great joke. "Really, kid, where is that dog hiding?"

I thought for a minute. "He's not here," I said. "I haven't seen him since that day."

"Oh, I see. You only borrow him when you need him?" Marvin asked.

"Hey, Marvin," Jake said. "Maybe he wishes for the dog to come."

"Yeah! Maybe. Kind of like Santa. Is that what you did when Barry took your bike? You wished the dog would find it? I see you have a new one."

"Hey, Paul," Jake said, "do you think if I pick you up and toss you right out there in the water that your wish dog will come and save you?" Jake reached around Marvin and grabbed my shirt. I pulled away to the sound of a button popping off. Jerry sat looking at them with his big eyes, while they talked, never saying a word—until Jake grabbed me. Then Jerry stood up slowly and picked up his fishing pole and mine. He reeled then in, hook, line, sinker, and bait. He tied the ends off with a rubber band, remaining calm as if nothing was wrong. Marvin and Jake never even looked at him. He walked over and handed my fishing pole to me. I thought it was time to go. He walked about four feet away from them. With both hands locked on his pole handle, he started swinging it, first at Marvin and then at Jake, back and forth. The whiplike, action along with the weight and hook, started cutting valleys in their skin. Jerry had to use every muscle in his body to hit them that hard. They tried to get away as he jumped around like he was made of rubber.

Well, I wasn't even sure why, but my fear of the bullies was gone, for now anyway. My best friend was fighting for me, and I had to join in. Marvin and Jake tried to back up, but they were not as fast as I thought they would be. I guess carrying around all that weight, those big leather boots and chains, slowed them down. Jake fell down as he tried to dodge the pole, first to one knee and then to both. I didn't have time just then to watch Jerry, but he moved like a sword fighter, and I followed. Marvin got a hold of Jerry's pole with one hand and stopped him from swinging it at him for a second. But his mistake was in trying to cover his face, which now had traces of blood flowing from it. He didn't see me coming as he grabbed the end of Jerry's pole and got a handful of hook. I left him, knowing how really out of shape he was. He was breathing hard and moving slow, holding his right hand in his left and screaming out in pain. I hit him five times, once for every time he tried to stop me. I jumped around him like I was fighting for my life, and now that I think about it, I guess I was. Jake was going to throw me in the Lincoln Park lagoon.

Jake was just about to stand up when he grabbed for my arm as I worked over Marvin. Then Jerry hit him in the back of his head with the handle of his pole, reel and all. Jake's blood was warm as it hit me in the back of my head. He went down again. I think Jake has the brand name of that fishing pole embedded in his head.

Well, the noise started to bring people yelling and screaming, but I guess I had so much anger built up in me from these guys picking on me all through school that I didn't want to quit. Jerry had to grab me and tell me that Marvin and Jake had enough and were trying to get away. By the time my senses came back, the two of them were just about out of sight. They were sure moving fast now. "Wow! Look at them go!" I yelled. Then I heard yelling and laughing. As I turned, I saw a crowd of people gathered behind Jerry and me. They started clapping, That's when I started to realize, for the first time, that these guys only looked like high school kids. They sure didn't act like them.

Jerry and I gathered up our stuff and headed home. We didn't talk too much until we were about halfway home, when I started to laugh, even though I didn't think I found any of this very funny. And I knew these guys wouldn't give up. I even watched for them while Jerry and I were going home. Jerry just looked at me for a while, and then it hit him the same way. The rest of the way home we walked our bikes and refought the whole fight. I think I told him ten times about when he hit Jake with the handle of that fishing pole, saying that I'd like to see the brand name that was left on his head.

"Paul!" Jerry said, while we were laughing so hard. "I know you thought I went nuts back there, but I really got scared when Jake said he was going to throw you in the water and then grabbed you. You're my best friend, and I know you can't swim that well. And, Paul, there was no Black Dog there to save you. And you know I can't swim that well either. There was only one way to keep that tub of lard from throwing you in the Lincoln Park lagoon."

"I know that, Jerry. And thanks," I said, "but you know they'll be back."

"Yeah! But this time there's two of us," Jerry said. "And you know what they say: two heads are better than one."

"Yeah! But there might still be five of them," I said.

"One more thing Paul," Jerry said, "why didn't you just tell them the dog was somewhere close?"

"Because I know them, Jerry. They would have punched me in my face just to see if there was a dog there to come to my rescue, and when they found out there was no dog, oh boy! I would have been dead or in the water."

"Yeah, I guess you're right," Jerry said. "But maybe they won't bother us anymore now that we fought back."

"I'd like to believe that, Jerry, but I'm sure that's not true. In fact, I think things may just get worse."

CHAPTER 11

The Bullies' Nightmare

Well, our fishing trip was interrupted by our good friends, and then our weekend was interrupted by the next day of rain. It was Jerry's turn to spend the night at my house, because his mom and dad were going to be gone all day Monday, until late. Mom picked us up Sunday evening, but before going home she had a few things to do. The rain had slowed for a while, but now it was worse than ever. "Where are we going, Mom?"

"We have to pick Grandma up at her friend's house and take her home. Grandpa was going to do it, but I had to pick you up, so I said I'd do it so that he wouldn't have to drive. It wasn't raining much when I left, or your dad would have come."

By the time we got there and had Grandma in the car it was starting to get dark. Also, it was still raining. We headed back to the house, but as we turned left off Mohawk onto Clark Street, we heard a loud crash and we all got hit with glass from the windshield exploding. Mom drove off the street over the curb onto the sidewalk and slammed on the brakes just before hitting a fence. Only a little glass hit us, but the window was smashed. Grandma was in the back seat with Jerry, and she was screaming. Mom jumped out of the car, ran around to my side, and opened the back door to check on Grandma. "Mom, are you okay?" she shouted.

Grandma was yelling at the top of her lungs, "Oh my God, what happened?"

"Are you hurt, Grandma?" Jerry shouted, while he tried to hold her still.

Mom checked Grandma over and found no blood. Then she looked at me, now standing in the rain behind her. "Are you boys okay?" Jerry shook his head yes to me, and I answered a quick, "We're fine, Mom, but you won't believe what just happened."

She stood up straight as if the rain had ended. "Paul! What are you talking about?" she said with that stern voice of hers while the rain ran down her face.

"Mom, when I jumped out of the car after you, to check on Gram, I saw two of the bullies from school, Marvin and Jake, standing over there. They took off, but I know it was them. Then, Mom, you know that big black dog I had the dream about and the big black dog that took Barry off my bike?"

"Yeah!" Mom said.

"Well, Mom, it's the same dog. And I'm sure, Mom. Black Dog was out there after them."

"Are you sure, Paul?"

"I'm sure, Mom. I'm only eleven, so I still have good eyes. And it's not that dark out yet. I think they must have thrown something at the windshield." Jerry was back in the car keeping Grandma calm. He couldn't hear because of the rain. As Mom and I talked, the police sirens got closer. People came out with umbrellas and blankets to cover us up. Our light coats were soaked, so the blankets helped.

Then we heard screaming coming from a distance. Everyone stopped talking. Jerry jumped out of the car and ran over by me. "Did you hear that, Paul?"

"Yeah! I sure did, and I think I know who it is." The police sirens were getting closer, but still we heard the screams.

While Mom checked on Gram, I took a flashlight from the car. I told Mom, "We'll be right back." She tried to object, but I slipped back into the crowd, pulling Jerry by the arm as I went. Then I took off toward the screams with Jerry on my heels.

I saw the police cars pull up at the car as I dropped my blanket and broke into a hard run. The screams got louder as I entered the alley by Mario's store. The rain was still coming down but had slowed to a steady drizzle. I walked hard and fast this time, because the screams had now turned to moans. I shut the flashlight off as I walked, so I could see them before they saw me. Jerry said nothing until we hit the alley and heard the moans and now a loud growl.

"What's going on back there, Paul?"

"You'll see, and you still won't believe." Not that far down the alley, we got a great surprise, through the dim lights that lit the rear doors of the stores and restaurants. I turned the flashlight on and found Marvin lying on the ground with nothing on his body but his underwear and one heavy black boot. His big fat belly looked like a shiny jack-o'-lantern with only one eye as the flashlight beam hit him. Our greatest surprise came when we saw Black Dog standing over him, with what seemed to be clothing material in his mouth. Plus there was clothing spread all over the alley. But something was wrong. Now I may have just turned eleven a short time ago, but I knew there were more clothes here than one person could wear. I looked around, but other than Black Dog, Marvin, Jerry, and me, I couldn't see anyone else. I knew I'd seen Jake when I jumped out of the car, but I figured he must have gotten away with not much more than his life. I walked over to Marvin and put the light right in his face. Even through the light rain, we could see he was now the one with tears in his eyes.

His first words were something I'd never expected to hear from him. He begged, "Please! Get that dog away from me. I'll do anything, just keep him away."

"I will," I said, "if you tell me why you did that to our car tonight. You broke our windshield and made my mom wreck her car. You could have killed us."

"I didn't do anything!" he yelled. Black Dog lunged forward with that loud growl that even scared me, enough to make me back up. Jerry started to run, but I grabbed his arm. Black Dog dropped the clothes from his mouth and grabbed Marvin by the last remaining boot and gave it a quick tug, leaving Marvin now with only one dirty white sock and his underwear. Marvin let out a scream as if Black Dog had just ripped off his leg, I was sure everyone in Chicago heard him.

The boot was gone in a flash, flying through the air over Black Dog's head. It landed on top of that big red dumpster that Marvin had thrown my school bag in, by the Chinese restaurant. When the boot hit, a sound came from inside the dumpster. Jerry and I looked at each other for a moment, and I said that it was probably just a big rat. It reminded me that I didn't want to be here any longer than I had to be.

"Maybe you should try telling the truth from now on, unless you want to go to jail naked. Remember, you only have your underwear on right now. The next time you lie, you're going to be very embarrassed."

"Okay! Okay!" Marvin said. He pulled himself up into a ball, checking to see if he still had both legs. "We were out looking for girls." Black Dog lunged again, but this time Marvin screamed out a protest quickly. "I'm sorry!" he yelled. "We were looking for car parts to rob. You know, radios, hubcaps, fender skirts, and things like that."

"Yeah! Go on before Black Dog gets bored, because he really gets angry when he gets bored."

"Well, we saw you get out of that car on Mohawk and help that old lady into it, so we waited down the street. We only threw a few rocks at your car," he yelled, "only to scare you. We didn't mean to make you crash."

I looked at Jerry and said, "That's what they always say when they get caught trying to hurt someone, 'We didn't mean to.' By the way, Marvin, that old lady is my grandmother. Now, tell us who was with you, as if we don't know."

"I can't tell you that. Even if that dog eats me right now," Marvin said, "I won't tell you."

"Wow! That's great," Jerry said. "We can leave Black Dog here with him and we can go home and get out of this rain." Jerry grabbed my arm and started to pull me back down the alley. Marvin started to scream again Then Black Dog started to bark, something I'd never heard before. And now I knew why too. He had a bark so loud that I think it hurt his ears as much as it hurt ours. He shook his head rapidly left to right as to say, *Wow! That hurts,* and then he walked slowly over to the big red dumpster while keeping an eye on Marvin. Then I realized what he was doing, as if now I could read his mind like he read mine the day he saved me from that beating when Marvin and the boys jumped me.

"Marvin!" I said. "You better stay where you are. I can't be responsible for anything if you get up." Black Dog turned to look him right in the eyes.

"Please, I'll stay right here, just keep him away from me," he said, with tears still rolling from his eyes. Then Black Dog turned his head toward me and looked me right in the eyes, as if to say, *Watch him.* I nodded an "okay." Then he headed over to the big red dumpster, this time quietly. He stood so tall on his hind legs that his head reached high over the top of the dumpster, the one that I'd had to stand on a five-gallon bucket just to see inside. He stood there for about a minute, with his front paws right on top, sniffing from one end to the other. Then he moved to the left end of the dumpster and started to bark that bark that only he could bark, over and over. I had to cover my ears, and as I did so I looked at Marvin and Jerry, who were now covering their ears too. Black Dog barked maybe ten times, shaking his head violently left to right with every bark. All of a sudden the lid on the right side of the dumpster flew open with great force. Marvin's boot, which was still sitting on that lid, went airborne again and hit the light over the rear door of the Chinese restaurant, causing a bright flash and then leaving that area in total darkness as the light went up in smoke.

I pointed my flashlight at the lid and out popped Jake. I yelled at Jerry, "Look, a jack-in-the-box."

Jerry yelled, "You mean a Jake-in-the-box, don't you, Paul?" Black Dog lunged at Jake, and Jake fell back into the dumpster of slop. Jerry and I laughed like never before. The smell was worse than I remembered.

I yelled to Jake, "Come out, or the dog, as big as he is, will reach in and pull you out."

He started screaming, "Keep that monster away from me! He was trying to kill me. That's how I got in here in the first place." Black Dog stood growling at him for a while, and then I waved the dog down, not knowing if he would do what I wanted. He got down, and moved back from the dumpster and stood at my side. I slowly lifted my hand high enough to rest it on his back, feeling the two layers of hair that Randolph had told us about at the library. Then a familiar voice came from behind us. It was Mario.

"Mario, did you see what happened here?" I asked in a very loud and rushed voice.

"Slow down, Paul, you're starting to sound like your hurried friend here." He nodded and said hello to Jerry.

"Well, I saw that dog strip those two boys clean of their clothes and toss them around like rag dolls in just a few seconds as they tried to get away. But after hearing what that guy rolled up in a ball over there said about throwing rocks at your car and the wreck, I'm sure I'll never say that again. I didn't come out, though, because that is the biggest dog I have ever seen in my life. Not to mention that bark being the loudest I've ever heard."

"Mario, that's the dog I asked you about when I came to your store that day." "Well, he is big and black, I'll say that. You know, Paul, it was so dark out here that I couldn't see much. And as black as he is, I sure couldn't see him at all, if you know what I mean," he said with a smile on his face. I just smiled back and nodded. "But I heard these boys yelling and I called the cops. I think I was on the phone when most of this happened. Sorry I can't tell you more." And again he said, "If you know what I mean, Paul," and smiled. He told us, "If the police know too much about that dog, from all of us, they'll have the dog catchers on full alert tonight and tomorrow. And that won't be good."

"What about the school bullies there?" I asked.

"Well, from what I know about them and from what I heard him say about throwing rocks at your car, the police won't care much about what they say about a dog, do you think, Paul?"

"I sure hope not, Mario."

The police cars pulled into the alley with their sirens blaring and their lights flashing. Their headlights lit up the whole place as Jake started to exit the dumpster. We stood back as Mario rested one hand on Jerry's shoulder and then put his other hand around the back of my neck, giving each of us a slight pull backward to his store. We watched Jake climb out of the dumpster while yelling about this giant dog that had chased him and his friend down the street and into the alley and tried to kill them for no reason. His face and hair were covered with what my mom would call Chinese noodles. Everyone started laughing, even the police. He hit the ground and ran to the police car, trying to open the door. He wasn't wearing much more than Marvin. His belly was as bare as Marvin's, but at least he still had his pants on. Only one leg was gone, and so was his big black belt and the chains that use to hang from it. He had no boots, but at least he still had both socks.

As another police car rolled into the alley and came to a halt, Marvin was trying to stand. The first policeman to arrive was trying to tell Jake, with a very stern voice, that he could not get in the car. "He said you have to wait for the paramedics to come and check you out. And young man," the policeman said, "you smell really bad, and you have things hanging from your body and your hair. I think it's garbage." Marvin was pointing down past Mario's store and yelling about a big black dog that had attacked them and then took off down the alley when they pulled in.

The policeman asked us if we had seen a big dog run down the alley. Mario was quick to answer, "What dog, Officer?" I looked around, but as always Black Dog was gone.

"That's not a good thing for that dog, guys," Mario said to me and Jerry in a very soft voice while Jake was yelling at the cop. "That alley is closed off because they're building a new apartment building down there. There is no way out. And I'll tell you something else, if they don't find him, then we're all going to start believing in magic."

Jerry and I snapped our heads up to look at Mario. Even in the dark alley we could see a smile from ear to ear on Mario's face. I heard the cop say to Marvin, "There's nowhere for that dog to go, so we'll get him when the dog catchers get here, if there really was a dog. But you and your friend have to go to the hospital and get checked out. And if the doctors find any bites on you and we don't find that dog, you know what that means? You get to get rabies shots." And he smiled right in Marvin's face. "Ten of them," he said, "right in the belly. One for every day for ten days." And he smiled again. "And the needle they use is about a foot long."

Jerry and I, hearing that, looked at each other and smiled a big smile.

Mario was talking to another cop. He told him about the bullies throwing rocks at Mom's car and causing an accident. The cop said that he had just come from there and that he knew Marvin and the boys very well.

After the police got done with all of us, Marvin and Jake went in the ambulance to the hospital. Jerry and I got a ride in the cop car to the hospital, where Mom and Grandma went for a checkup.

Jerry's mom and dad were there waiting with my mom and dad and grandpa. Jerry and I sure were in big trouble. While we all waited to find out if Grandma was going to get to go home that night, I sat trying to tell this most unbelievable story, that all started at school with five bullies. Mom was really mad at me for running off after the accident, as I expected. "But I really thought we would get back before we were missed," I told her. I stuttered out what I could about Black Dog helping me out on my way home from school, and Jerry tried to help, but we were still in big trouble. The doctor came into the room where we were waiting and told Mom she could go home but that Gram had to stay the night. Grandpa stood and started to say something, but the doctor said, "Nothing's wrong, but I want her to rest overnight. Just going out in the weather and night air right now would wear her out." Mom and Grandpa went in to say their goodbyes first, and then Dad went in, as Jerry and I waited.

We were all just about to leave the hospital when Mario came through the front door. He sure helped us out. He was able to tell my parents what happened a lot better than Jerry and I could. He told then about these boys who caused trouble for all the store owners around this part of town. Mario told them how he and I had first met in the alley, and how the bullies were looking for me. Mario told them how he saw Marvin through my school bag in the dumpster and how the black dog seemed to herd them to that same dumpster for a taste of Chinese food. That sure made everyone laugh. He also told Mom that the police said there was enough evidence that the boys threw rocks at her car and broke the window. But even though Marvin initially had said they did it, he changed his story in the ambulance.

"I told them I heard Marvin say they did it," Mario said, "but once they were in the ambulance, they said they never did that or said that." Then Mario said, "If that black dog hadn't chased them tonight after they hit your car with those rocks, no one would have ever known they were the ones who caused the accident that put you all here tonight, except for Paul, and no one would have believed him after Marvin and Jake changed the story around."

Grandpa stood to face Mario, and said, "After hearing this story about these bullies and this dog, I have to believe that Paul is a very lucky boy. I'd hate to think what would have happened to him in the past if this black dog hadn't been around. I'm like all of you right now." He turned to face Mom and Dad and Jerry's parents. "I'm wondering where this dog came from and why he chose Paul to take care of, and like you all, I'm grateful he did. And I'm sure going to look for the answers." The look on Grandpa's face, as well as his soft voice, was enough to make everyone listen. Once he was finished, he sat down in silence and stared at the floor.

"By the way, Paul," Mario said very quietly, almost looking like he wanted to cry, "soon after you left, the dog catchers got there. There were four of them with those poles, you know, with the ropes on them for catching things, and a few cops. They said if there was a dog and the dog went that way, it would be trapped." Mario said, "A dog catcher told me, with his cocky voice, 'We'll get him.' They started their search of the whole alley. That's why I took so long to get here. I knew you'd want to know about Black Dog." Everyone seemed to hold their breath as Mario spoke. Then he hesitated. My eyes were like daggers as I stared at Mario. I think he hesitated just to be funny. "They don't know how, but that dog was gone," Mario said. Everyone in that room let out a sigh of relief, including my mom. Jerry and I jumped up and down, yelling "all right" with our hands in the air, until my mom reminded us, with a smile on her face, that we were in a hospital. Mario said, "The cops said the only way out of that alley was to fly out, or climb out, because of the construction, and the other end was fenced off with a ten-foot-high wire fence. The cops aren't even sure now if this big black dog story the boys told them is real. The cops think the boys made it up because they knew you saw them by the car when it got hit.

"I couldn't tell them anything about a dog," Mario said, "because I was on the phone calling them. It must have left before I came out, or maybe it was never there." As Mario spoke, he looked right into my eyes, and through his seriousness I could see him saying to the cop in that alley, "What dog?" I had to smile. "They said they'll have to wait for the doctors' reports on booth boys. The only way to tell is to see if those boys have been bitten. But I can tell you this, the paramedics said there were no marks on those boys to show that they were attacked by any dog that had great big razor-sharp teeth, but they did have skinned arms and knees from the concrete and gravel they fell on in the alley. They said it looked more like those boys were fighting with each other and didn't want to tell anyone, so they made up this dog story.

"Oh yeah, Paul, the boys told the police that this dog belongs to you."

"Yes, sir! I've heard that story before," I said in what my mom calls my cocky way. "But to be truthful, Mario, like Grandpa said, I don't know where he comes from and I sure don't know where he goes. But I am sure glad he's there when I need him."

"I'm sure by the look on everyone's faces around you right now," Mario said, "they're glad he was there too."

CHAPTER

12

Black Dog Dies

WELL, NOW MORE THAN ever, I was a prisoner. Mom wasn't sure about the black dog story either. Oh, she believed my story about a dog being there when I needed him, but she didn't believe a dog could strip all the clothes off those boys without leaving any teeth marks on them and then go down the alley and disappear where there was nowhere to go. Mom said, "I'm not sure he'll ever be there again when you need him. And if not, these boys will hurt you, Paul. They sure are in a lot of trouble since they ran into you and that black dog. And they sure won't let it go that easy."

Now I'm not sure what happened to get me into the spot I was in right now, but I knew it wouldn't get any better unless I found out where Black Dog came from and where he went, and most of all unless I answered the question that everyone had: Why me? I needed to get to the library and had to go with Grandpa or not at all, because Mom thought I needed a bodyguard.

Grandpa parked right next to the front door. As we got out of the car, we heard a voice from behind us. Grandpa yelled, "Hey, Paul! I think he's talking to you."

"Yes, sir," I said. I turned to see Randolph walking up to Grandpa's side of the car. Then I realized that Grandpa had his hand up waving for Randolph to come over to him. As Randolph approached Grandpa, he got a look on his face as if the third degree was next. "Grandpa, he's the man we're here to see," I said. Then Grandpa's mean face turned to a smile. Grandpa and I said hello to Randolph, and the two of them introduced themselves. Then I told Randolph a little about why we were there. Grandpa told him about the bullies and why he was with me. Randolph waited until we were all done talking, but I could see a smirk on his face just waiting to be set free.

"Well, young man," Randolph said, "the other night I was on my way home from work in a hellacious rainstorm when, I believe, I saw that black dog of yours."

"Where?" I said enthusiastically.

"Well, I believe he was chasing two boys who were running for their lives down Armitage Avenue."

"Grandpa!" I yelled. 'That's the night Marvin and Jake took off after they hit Mom's car with those rocks."

"I know, Paul," Grandpa said, putting one hand on my shoulder, "but don't explode on us here."

"Follow me," Randolph said. He smiled and gave Grandpa a look that I knew meant, *He's a kid.* Grandpa nodded his head back at Randolph, as if to say, *I know.*

Inside the building we greeted the librarian and made our way back to where Randolph had taken us before, to show us the newspaper clipping of Black Dog and the emperor.

"You know, Paul, this Black Dog thing of yours is not so unusual. There are a lot of stories about animals that have come to the rescue of people all the way back to when newspapers started.

"I have one here you won't believe, about a big black bear that fought off a very large pack of hungry wolves that were trying to attack a small family of Indians in the 1870s. It lasted three days, and the bear never left. When it was over, the wolves had lost and the bear was gone and was never seen again. The strange thing about this story was that there were no black bears, or any other bears for that matter, ever seen in that part of the upper desert of California. You can read all day of animals just like your black dog. But what I want to show you is a story about a big black dog that I think might have something to do with the emperor's dog, the story that I showed you and your friends when you were here last." He pulled out a clipping and laid it on the table, and there the Akita was again, only this time it was a much better picture of Black Dog, as plain as if I were standing in front of him in that alley behind Mario's store, the first time I saw him. I felt a cold chill run up and down my back as I read the story beneath the picture. Then I lost my breath for a moment. Grandpa grabbed me as I started to fall to my knees.

The story read as follows:

> A school bus loaded with children on their way home from summer camp were saved from a tragic accident.
>
> A large black dog ran out in front of a school bus today loaded with children and brought the bus to a sudden halt. The children were not injured, as the bus driver swerved and stopped to miss the dog. But the big black dog was hit by a car that, while speeding through a red light, would have surely hit the bus, but hit the dog instead. The dog was killed, and the driver of the car was injured after hitting the large dog and taken to the hospital. Later police said that the emperor of Japan is missing dog, shown in the picture above, resembling the dog at the scene. The emperor's dog had gotten out of his cage while being transported back home to Japan after the emperor's visit last week.

"How could this be the same dog," Grandpa asked Randolph, "if he was killed?"

"Well, read on," Randolph said, "and you'll see how there are things in this life that don't always have an explanation."

The next paragraph read as follows:

> The black dog was pronounced dead at the scene and was taken to the Sheffield Animal Hospital for the owners to claim. It was placed in a truck and transported with care

> as any hero should have been, but when the rear doors of the truck were opened at the animal hospital, the two men in attendance got a great surprise. When they swung the doors open, the big black dog was up on all fours and staring them right in the eyes. The men told a reporter later that they were sure the dog was smiling at them just before it jumped out of the truck, to the street, and was gone in a flash. The attendants said they never had a chance to stop the dog. They also said this dog weighed somewhere around two hundred pounds and ran like a racehorse. They'd even needed help loading him into the back of the truck. Police say they will continue investigating and searching for the dog.

My heart went into full motion and I could breathe again. As I finished reading the story, I looked at the date on the top of the page. "Hey!" I yelled. "Look at this. This school bus accident happened the day I was born. That's my birthday, Grandpa."

Randolph looked at the date, and read, "July 10, 1945."

"I think I know where you're going with this," Grandpa said to Randolph. "I wonder if we can get a copy of the police report and see what time that wreck happened."

"We don't need to," Randolph said. "I'll call the paper. I have a friend over there. She should be able to tell us from the old police report. I'm sure they keep them." Randolph said. "Paul, what time were you born?"

"I'm sorry, sir, I really don't know. Grandpa, do you know?"

"No," he said. "Not exactly, but I know it was midafternoon."

"Paul, I think we may have the answer to why this dog has chosen you to protect," Randolph said.

Well, it didn't take long for us to get an answer from the lady at the paper. Randolph thanked her as he wrote something down on a piece of paper he'd found on the desk. Then he hung up. "Well, Paul, now you need to call your mom," he said.

Mom had just gotten home from work when the phone rang. She

was out of breath. She sure didn't understand why I was so interested in what time I was born, but she told me anyway. "Has this got something to do with that dog thing of yours? And where is Grandpa?" She sounded a little angry, but I think any time she had to think of the bullies, she became hard to deal with.

"He's right here, Mom."

"Well, let me talk to him." I didn't say goodbye. I just handed the phone to him.

While Grandpa talked to Mom, I looked at Randolph and told him what Mom had said. "I was born at 3:10 p.m." Randolph's eyes got very large. As Grandpa spoke to Mom, he kept his eyes on us. When he saw Randolph's eyes, he said a hurried goodbye to Mom and hung up. I was sure Mom had no chance to say her goodbye, but I was also sure that Grandpa could get away with it. We both looked at Randolph.

"That school bus accident was at 3:10 p.m., the same time Paul was born," he said to Grandpa. We all stood silent for a moment. Then Randolph said, "Now I'm not sure if you two know anything about life transformation, but sometimes, as I said before, things can't always be explained. As this dog lost his life, I think your being born at that same time, Paul, had something to do with his being revived. You might think I'm crazy, but don't ask me to explain just yet. There's just too many things that have happened to you, Paul, to let this thing go without looking real hard at. I'll need some time to search it out, but I'm sure the answers are in this library. Now I know you two have a lot of questions, but I have to get to work, or else I won't have a job at this library to find out the answers."

We all said our goodbyes, and Grandpa and I started out the door. Then I stopped and turned back to Randolph. "Sir, can I ask you a favor?"

"Sure," Randolph said. "Anything."

"Well! Can you forget about seeing Black Dog chasing Marvin and Jake, please?"

"What black dog? Where? When?" he said. We all laughed. And then Grandpa and I left.

The Stooges Look Bad Again

CHAPTER 13

THE SUMMER VACATION WAS about to end. Another three weeks and back to school, which was not something I was looking forward to.

"The last time I saw Jake," Jerry said, "his sister Mary had been at his house a few days before, and she said that Jake had been in trouble all his life."

"Wow!" I said to Jerry. "All twelve years."

He laughed and said, "No, thirteen now," and then he kept on talking. "She said that Jake was told by the court that if he didn't straighten up, he would be on his way to a long, lonely life in a jail cell. She said Jake laughed at that after he left the court, and he really got his dad mad. Jake can't leave the house until school starts, and then he has to go to school and get back home. Mary said her dad is looking into military school for Jake. Everyone thinks that's the best thing for him."

"Him!" I said. "What about our school? And me? I'm the one he wants to kill."

Jerry stopped talking and stared at me. "Are you done feeling sorry for yourself, Paul?"

I told him, "Change places with me anytime, Jerry." He shook his head no and smiled at me. "I thought so," I said. "What about Marvin?" I asked.

"Well, Mary said they talk on the phone a lot but they can't see each other or else they go back to the pokey. Jake doesn't say much when anyone's around, but she knows he's up to something, because he's too secretive on the phone when he's talking to Marvin and the rest of the cons he hangs out with."

The next day I was waiting for Jerry at my house. When he got there I was supposed to call Grandpa to pick us up. We were all going to the Lincoln Park lagoon to do a little fishing. Mom was okay with this fishing trip without putting up a fight, because my dad had reminded her I was getting older and needed a life. I still got that mom look that she gave me when Dad and I ganged up on her, as she called it.

The doorbell rang. I opened the door thinking it was Jerry, but to my very big surprise it was Jake, looking as mean as I had ever seen him. He stepped in fast and grabbed at my shirt. I heard that old familiar sound as my shirt ripped in his hand as I tried to get away. Jake reached for the door and slammed it with his other hand. I pulled away again, and this time I left Jake with a piece of my shirt balled up in his hand. I didn't get far, though. I turned into the corner of the living room, with no way out. Jake reached out and grabbed my hair, pulling me to him. I tried to fight him off, but he got a hold around my neck and started choking me. I was sure he would have killed me if I hadn't gotten hold of the lamp sitting on the end table. He knocked it over as he pulled me into the kitchen. I grabbed the lamp as it fell. He tried to get a better hold on me as I held on to the lamp with both hands. He lost his grip for the moment, and I broke loose in the kitchen with my back to the rear door. I faced him as I lifted the lamp to hit him. I felt the weight of the lamp become heavier and heavier. I couldn't move it over my head. Then I heard Marvin's cocky voice from behind me.

"Let go of the lamp, little man. If it gets broken, your mom will be real mad." I let go of the lamp, and turned to see Marvin and Sammy standing there laughing. Then Marvin threw the lamp across the kitchen. It hit the sink. As it exploded, he said, "Oops, I dropped it. You should always lock your doors, little man. You never know who might come in, especially when you have no guard dog on duty."

Oh boy! I thought to myself. Things were not going well right now, but I still had to take the time to think about the day when we all went to the kennel to find a dog for me and I went home empty-handed. Marvin and Sammy each held pieces of steel pipe and pointed them at me as Marvin talked. Jake just stood quietly and listened. "By the way, dog boy," Marvin said, "where is your brother dog today? As you can see, we are ready for him." They waved their pipes in my face.

"Oh, I don't think you really want to see him right now, Marvin. You have enough trouble now," I said.

Marvin said, "Well, if you mean because we came in your house, there's no trouble for us. You invited us in." Looking at this friends, he said, "Right, guys?"

They all laughed and said, "*Ya!*"

While Marvin talked, someone outside in front of the house whistled. They all froze, except Marvin. "That Little Hank sure can whistle," he said. He grabbed me by my neck and told me not to make a sound. Then the front doorbell rang.

A loud voice rang out. We all knew it was Jerry. He yelled again and the bell rang again. Then he yelled, "I'm going around back."

By this time Marvin had the back door opened and was ready to make a break for the alley. But he changed his mind when he found out it was only Jerry. "Close the door," he said. "We need to talk to him too. He wasn't very nice at the park with that fishing pole. We still owe him too!" He looked at Jake, who remained silent. Marvin yelled, "Sammy! Hide behind the door and grab Jerry when he comes in." Jerry came in as he always did when he knew my parents were not home, very loud and very fast. He opened the door so fast that he smashed Sammy between the door and the wall. Sammy's nose exploded, pouring blood as he fell to his knees. Marvin pulled me to him and hung on tighter than ever. Jerry needed some time to figure this whole thing out.

"What's this?" Jerry asked as he saw Sammy screaming and bleeding, trying to straighten up behind the now half-open kitchen door. "Holy smoke, did I just do that?" Jerry asked. I started to laugh beyond uncontrollably. Jake was holding his mouth with both hands as though he was going to be able to hold his laughter in, but that didn't last for long. He bent over to hide the laughter as it exploded from his mouth.

He was laughing so hard that he ran out of the house and down the stairs to the backyard. I tried to get away and get outside too, but Marvin was hanging on tight. He sure didn't find any of this as funny as Jake and I did.

By this time Sammy had grabbed a towel off the kitchen counter to stop the bleeding. He was so mad that he wanted to kill Jerry. The noise between Jake and me laughing and Sammy yelling from pain was so loud that Hank came out of hiding and ran up the stairs just as Marvin was trying to leave.

"We need to get out of here," Marvin said, "before someone calls the cops. But before we leave, you better know this, Paul. We know where that black dog is, and we plan to get rid of him for the last time. By the way, Paul, you better clean up this house before your mom and dad get home, and think up a good story without including our names if you ever want to see that dog again. I'll let you know where to be and what time." Marvin grabbed Sammy by his bloody shirt and pulled him out the door. Hank followed, slamming the door behind him. I ran and locked both doors. Jerry, still looking as though he was dreaming, didn't say a word as he grabbed a chair near the kitchen table and sat down very slowly, his eyes staring at me and looking like large dinner platters. He was breathing slow, hard, and very loud. After a while, he turned his head toward the back door, looking at the blood that had now run down to the floor. He stuttered out a few words I couldn't understand, but I said nothing. I just stared back at him, waiting for him to get his composure back.

"Paul, I asked you if I did that."

"Yes, Jerry, you did that to Sammy. He was hiding behind the door waiting to grab you. They were still mad about us making them look bad at the park with that fishing pole thing, but again, they seem to have gotten the worst of it. You would think by now they would have learned that they are not the gangsters they think they are. In fact, they seem more like the four stooges." Jerry didn't laugh at that, though. He just shook his head yes as if to agree with me.

I left Jerry sitting in the kitchen to get his head straight while I went into the living room to assess the damage. I knew Marvin was right about one thing: I couldn't tell Mom and Dad that they'd been here, because if they really did find Black Dog, they would hurt him if they got the chance. I needed to clean up and think up a real good story and get Jerry to get it straight and go along with it. Not only that, but also if Mom knew that these guys had been in our house, she would go crazy and start another world war.

Well, it was easy to put the living room back in order, except for the lamp. It sure was a mess. As for the kitchen, the blood was mostly on the door and the floor, so I started to clean it up. *I sure wish I could get Jerry to do this,* I thought, *but he is still not himself.* A strong stomach, a lot of rags from the basement, and a lot of dish soap made the living room look like new, or so I thought. I cleaned up the broken glass from the lamp, which was made of metal but had glass inside it, and swept the floor. Everything looked good except that poor lamp.

As I worked on trying to straighten out the shade, Jerry had come back to this world. He came in to the living room. I hated to admit it, but, I had no time to baby him right now. I said, "Get a bulb out of that closet and put it in here." About that time I heard the front door being unlocked, and I knew it was Grandpa. I stood with my hands frozen to the lampshade, motionless, as Grandpa walked through the door and closed it without taking his eyes off me.

"I think you guys had a mishap," he said in his own funny way. "What did you guys do now?"

I knew I had to think fast, but I didn't want to lie to him. He was Grandpa, and my best friend. When I needed anything, such as help or answers, I knew I could count on him, But I knew if I told him the truth, he would have to tell my mom and dad, and then the trouble would start. And if Marvin really knew where Black Dog was, he would be hurt or dead. At any rate, he would be gone forever. So I lied. "Well, Grandpa, Jerry and I are tired of bullies pushing us around, so we watched wrestling the other night and were trying some of the things we saw."

"I think you would have had more room outside," he said. "Right, guys?"

"Yes, sir," we said, one after the other.

"As for this lamp, I think your mom is going to be very unhappy. She really likes this thing. Your dad will be glad it's gone but not very happy about the way it went. But, as always, Grandpa might be able to help."

"Wow! How, Grandpa?"

"Well, this lamp was a set of two, which I, like your father, never liked. It took me forever to get your grandmother to buy new lamps, which cost me plenty. You see boys, new lamps came with the new living room furniture I had to buy. So the mate to this lamp wound up in the basement in a corner in a box so that Grandma wouldn't see it and put it in the bedroom or somewhere else I'd have to look at it for the rest of my life. I'll be right back. But first one thing, boys. You will remember, won't you, that you owe me bigtime for this. And I think from now on when we go fishing, you will be baiting all my hooks and cleaning all my fish."

"Grandpa, for you it will be a pleasure," I said.

Then Jerry said, "Grandpa, thanks! From now on we will do our fighting outside."

I looked at Jerry with admiration. He sure knew how to be adult when he had to.

The lamp worked out well. We cleaned up the one Grandpa brought us and then tossed the broken one, along with the bent shade, in the trash can out behind the garage and covered it with other trash. Then we made sure everything was perfect in the house. Then the three of us went fishing. And yes, that day we, meaning Jerry and I, started baiting all Grandpa's hooks and cleaning all his fish.

CHAPTER

14

The Hero

ONE WEEK LATER, I had just walked into the house and the phone rang. It was Randolph. He said in a hurried voice, "I need to talk to you and your parents. Are they home?"

"No. Mom will be home soon, and Dad will get back a little later."

"Well, you tell them I'll be over about six. And have your grandpa there too, if he can make it. I have a few things you all need to see."

Mom and Dad were both home when Randolph arrived. I introduced them and wasted no time trying to find out what he had for us. "Is Grandpa coming?" Randolph asked.

"Soon," my dad said.

"Then let's wait for him. I'm sure he'll be interested in what I found."

Mom made a big pot of coffee and put out some donuts. She said, "This might be a long night." Grandma and Grandpa arrived soon thereafter, and after more introductions, we all sat at the kitchen table, staring at Randolph.

"Well, first of all, I have to ask this," Randolph said. "When I last saw you, Paul, and you, Grandpa, do you guys remember I told you that some things can't be explained? Well, I have some things you all need to see." He opened a box that held what looked like newspaper. "These are old newspaper clippings that I got from that friend of mine at the *Chicago News*. She said she knew we would be interested in them, so she dropped them off at the library. Let's start at the earliest date, July

13,1945, three days after that black dog saved that busload of kids, and of course three days after your birthday, Paul. I'll read them to you so you don't all need to."

The story read as follows:

> A large black dog foiled a robbery early last night when three men broke into Manson's Jewelry Store through the back door shortly after it had closed. While the robbers were filling their bags with jewelry and money from the safe, the owner returned. He unlocked the front door, and to his surprise found the robbers at work. One of the men subdued him by grabbing around the neck and throwing him to the floor. The robbers then ran for the back door to a waiting car.
>
> But as they started out the back door, the first man was hit by a large black dog, knocking him back into the store and onto his head, and ripping his shirt from his body in what the owner said was just a matter of seconds.
>
> The store owner said that as the other robbers turned and headed for the front door, the black dog jumped the one in the rear, also bringing him to his knees and tearing away his pants and shirt, leaving him in his mask, underwear, and boots. The man seemed to be dazed and couldn't move after being hit by that big black dog.
>
> The third robber made it out the front door after dropping his bag and almost got away, but he was also foiled by the black dog, when the owner quickly opened the door for the black dog to pursue him. Fifteen minutes later the robber was found three blocks down by the police, hiding in a large dumpster, completely

> naked and yelling, "Oh God, help me," as the police opened the top.
>
> The store owner said that the two robbers who were left in the store managed to get out the back door without their bags of loot, just after he heard a car race out of sight, leaving then without a ride. The police are now looking for the two men, one wearing black boots, a mask, and his underwear, and the other missing his shirt and with a large lump on his head. They are also looking for the lone driver who was involved.
>
> Police are still investigating. Police are also looking for this large black dog.

I sure wanted to speak, but Mom held up that almighty hand, and we all just listened to Randolph. "There's more here, Paul, dated July 14, 1945.

> While filling up her car late last night, a young woman was attacked by a tall man with dark glasses who forced her into his car. "As he climbed in behind me, I heard him scream louder than I was," she told police. "Then I saw a very large black animal pulling this man down the road like a rag doll, and tossing him from side to side. I thought he was being attacked by a bear. As I watched this animal tear the man's clothes from his body, I realized, *That's no bear,* but it sure was the biggest dog I had ever seen," the woman told police and reporters. "Then the dog let the man go, and the man was screaming at the top of his voice. The dog watched him crawl away like wounded prey. Then this dog came back to the car that I had been pushed into and was much too scared to get out of. He stood there looking at me. At first I thought he was coming for me,

> but as we looked eye to eye, it was like I could read his mind. He'd just come back to see if I was all right. Then he was gone." The police found the woman's kidnapper naked and hiding in a shallow ditch, not far away. Police say, "The only marks found on the man were from the lady's fingernails and from being pulled by something along the rough street."

"These stories go on and on, right up until the time you first saw the dog in that alley. But what's most important about these stories is that no one had ever heard of this dog until after the emperor lost his dog, and of course the next time was on your birthday when that bus accident happened. I've talked to a few people who specialize in life transformation, but they say it seems to be a little different in this case, because the dog died and you were born at about the same time. That's how it works as far as they know. But in this case, the dog seems to have come back to life. So it has become a bigger mystery. And one other thing, Paul. Do you remember ever seeing an old Oriental man with a long beard and long walking stick?"

My heart starting pounding. Trying to remain calm, I answered, "I do! I do! The day all five boys grabbed me on my way home. I took a different way home to get away, but they found me. The old man was walking the other way on the other side of the street, just before the boys grabbed me. He was tapping that stick on the ground as he walked. That was the first time Marvin and his boys met Black Dog. They would have beaten me to a pulp if Black Dog hadn't shown up."

"Was that the first time you had to worry about these boys hurting you?" Randolph asked.

"Well, yes. I thought they were just trying to scare me, like they do the rest of the kids at school. But they seemed to be getting meaner. They chased me one day, and I hit them with my book bag and was able to get away. That's how I met Mario. But I really didn't have time to be scared like the time on my way home when Black Dog showed up. And when Barry stole my bike, I was scared because I knew I would be in big trouble with my dad for not locking it up."

"Well," Randolph said, "I think we have solved some of this puzzle for now. But give me a little more time. After I meet with my friends again, we'll work on it some more."

"Randolph! What has this old man got to do with Paul and this dog?" my dad asked.

"A few of the people throughout the years whom this dog has helped out thought they had seen this same old bearded man in the area when the black dog came to their rescue. They said the old man carried a long walking stick and was tapping it on the ground as he walked, and shortly after, the black dog showed up. There are stories around that tell of this old man being left behind by the emperor to find his dog, because he was the dog's handler and trainer and was held responsible for losing him. Other than that, nobody seems to know anything about the old man.

"Well, I have to go now, but I'll keep in touch as things progress. Be careful, Paul. These guys won't like you too much when you're back at school. I'll leave these other clippings with you that we didn't get to read about Black Dog."

CHAPTER 15 The Countdown

I SAT ON THE front stairs of my house thinking of how nice it would be if we really could move away from here. Today was the start of the countdown to the beginning of school. Ten more days and then back to trouble. It seemed like Marvin and his boys did anything they wanted to and then lied their way out of it. They broke into places and stole what they wanted, stole bikes, beat up people, caused accidents, shot out windows, and did many other things I can't remember, but then they went to court and were sent back home to do it all over again. Maybe no one really cared about them and they knew it, so they didn't care what happened to themselves. My mom and dad would beat me with an inch of my life if they had to come and get me out of jail. And I wouldn't want to think of what my life would be like after that.

Well, I'd have to wait ten more days to see what happened. Until then I was still a prisoner thanks to Marvin and the boys. And what made me so mad was that they were free to roam the streets. The last time I saw Marvin, he told me he knew where Black Dog was, and he said he was going to hurt him.

Making a call to Jerry was the thing I had to do now. He could get his sister Patty to find out what the boys were up to and find out if maybe they really did know where Black Dog was. I really didn't think they wanted to run into Black Dog again, but knowing Marvin and Jake as well as I did, I thought they might try anything to show everyone that they really were nuts, even taking on Black Dog again.

The day after Jerry and I talked, he called me back with the news. Jake was on the phone and his sister Mary was upstairs listening to him talk to Marvin. Mary heard them plotting to rip off some store the following Saturday night. The were going to wait until all their parents were asleep and leave their houses. She said she heard Jake say he was going to sneak out his bedroom window about eleven and he would meet all of them under the Webster Street el. Jerry said he had Patty ask Mary if she had heard anything about Black Dog, but she said, :No, nothing."

Well, that is good news for me, I thought to myself. *I think so anyway. At least robbing a store will keep them out of my hair. And better than anything else, maybe they'll get caught and be out of my hair for good this time.*

Mary said she heard Jake hang up and then he came upstairs. She ran into the bathroom and closed the door fast but quietly. She said he was really mad. He asked her if she'd been listening to him on the phone. She told him she had just gotten up. He said, "I thought you stayed overnight at Patty's house?" Mary told him no, because she didn't feel well last night and had come home early. If he would have known she heard, he would have gone nuts on her and hurt her bad, and there was no one home to stop him.

As usual, my luck with these guys was running about the same as it always had. All the kids in the neighborhood were spending the day at the park. Some were fishing in the lagoon, and some were deep into a great baseball game. A few moms and dads were there to keep an eye on us. There was plenty of food and drinks laid out on the tables. Of course this time my bike and all the rest of the bikes were chained up. Dad had bought me a heavy chain and a padlock that would need to be blown off with dynamite if I lost the key. So we didn't have to worry about bikes being gone. All in all, the day was great. I was beginning to think Chicago wasn't such a bad place to grow up in. And maybe living in the country would be a little boring.

As the day came to an end, Jerry and I headed over to our bikes, but he grabbed my arm and looked at me with those eyes as big as platters, just like I had seen in my kitchen a few weeks before, when Sammy got a face full of my back door.

"What's wrong, Jerry?" I asked quickly.

"Do you see that paper on your bike?" he asked. "It wasn't there when we left our bikes there."

"Well, maybe it just blew up there with the wind," I said.

"Yeah, maybe, Paul, but I don't remember any wind that strong today."

"Well, only one way to find out. Let go of my arm and I'll get it." He released me slowly, and we walked over to our bikes.

At first I thought someone was playing a joke on me. The white school paper was just hanging there, taped to the top bar of my frame. Jerry and I looked at each other for a moment. Then I reached down, grabbed the paper, and gave it a pull. It read, "We have the mutt, and if you want to see that black mutt of yours again, be at the Webster Street el at 11:00 p.m. Saturday. And if you tell your parents or the cops, the dog dies." I read the note to myself, not sure I wanted Jerry to be involved.

"What's it say?" he asked. I crumpled it up and started to put it in my pocket. I couldn't speak. Jerry grabbed my hand and held tight, and with his other hand he grabbed the note and pulled it out of my hand, leaving some of it behind. "It's Marvin, right, Paul?" Jerry asked as he turned to escape my reach.

"Yeah! But it's my worry. I don't want to get you in more trouble than we're in already."

"Well, what are friends for? It says the Webster Street el on Saturday—just what Mary told Patty, Paul. But now they say they have Black Dog."

"Well, to be honest, Jerry, I can't believe Black Dog has been around this long and has let these bullies catch him. You read all those stories about him, and you know he's dealt with people much smarter than them."

"Yeah, but I know you, Paul. You won't take the chance. You love that dog too much to let it go."

"Well, Jerry, if they have him now, they need to keep him caged, but I don't know of a cage big enough to hold that dog. At least nothing they have."

"Wait a minute, Paul. My dad had a welder at our house to build that gate in the backyard a few months ago and reinforce the garage door because someone broke in and stole his tools."

"Yeah! I remember, Jerry."

"Well, that welder was none other than Jake's dad."

"Yeah! You're right."

"Well, if he needed a big cage, his father sure could build it for him," Jerry said.

"Do you think he would do that?"

"Only if Jake lied to him," Jerry said.

"He's mad enough at Jake right now to let him stay in jail next time, Mary said. But we can have Patty call her again and find out if he built a cage for him."

"Even if you find out that they have Black Dog, Paul, how are you going to get out of the house Saturday night without getting caught?"

"I don't know, Jerry. My mom is a light sleeper, and I have never had to climb out my window. I'd probably fall and kill myself."

"Then you think that's out of the question, right, Paul?"

"Yeah," I said with a sneer. Jerry just laughed. "I'll think of something," I said. "I have to."

"Well, let me know, Paul. You're not going by yourself."

"No, Jerry, you can't go."

"Well, if I don't, you're not going either."

"This could be bad, Jerry. And no matter what, we'll be in big trouble with our parents."

"Like I said before, we'll find out together, won't we?" Jerry said. "Think of it this way, Paul. If they don't have Black Dog and they just want you there to beat you bloody, and Black Dog shows up, I sure don't want to miss that, not even with all the trouble I'll get in for being out late at night."

"That's a great thought, Jerry," I said, "but think of it this way. What if Black Dog doesn't show up, like in the kitchen and at the park?"

"Why do you always want to ruin my day, Paul?" This time I laughed.

We heard one of the moms come up behind us, telling us she needed our help packing up and saying that it was time to go home.

Our bike convoy ended as it started, back in the neighborhood, which should have been the end to a perfect day, but it wasn't for me. I didn't want to leave my house late at night and meet with these guys to let them beat me up, but Black Dog had saved me from them before and found my bike, and most of all he'd paid them back for wrecking Mom's car. I couldn't take a chance that they had him and would hurt him just because I was too scared to show up. No, I had no choice.

Mary the Spy

CHAPTER

16

JERRY CALLED ME BACK just after he got home from our bike convoy. "Paul," Jerry said, "Patty called Mary and asked her to ask her dad about the cage. But Paul, she already knew the answer. She said she was waiting for Jake to go to sleep so she could call us. He did build a cage for Jake. Just today. Jake told him he was going to raise dogs, train them, and sell them. Mary knew something was fishy when Jake told her dad that he would be better if he had something to do with his life. She said the cage is down in the garage. She watched her dad build it. And she said it's big, so big that Jake can stand up in it, and it has a gate on one end that goes all the way to the top. And it can be taken apart to move it just by lifting the sides and ends out of the cage floor. She also said there aren't any dogs in it now, but when she asked Jake today when he was getting his dogs, he said he had one coming soon. She also said he wasn't very friendly about it."

Well, that didn't come as a big surprise to me. I was sure they didn't have Black Dog, but I still was not sure they didn't know where to get him. Or how.

Thursday morning I woke up early with an idea that I thought might just work. Mom and Dad were in the kitchen getting ready for work. I called Jerry and told him to come over as soon as possible. "We need to talk, but not on the phone," I whispered.

"What's up, Paul?"

"Not on the phone, Jerry."

"Okay!" he said. "I'll be there."

Dad hurried out with a quick goodbye, and Mom took time to tell me the same thing she always told me when she left. "I'll call from work, Paul, but if you need anything—"

I interrupted, saying, "Call Grandpa, Mom, I know. Or call you at work."

"Paul! We need to talk about you stopping me from saying the things I as a mother need to say. I know you don't like me telling you the same thing over and over, but you have to admit, you and this dog thing is not easy to handle. And this thing with these bullies has changed our lives around here."

"Mom! I asked you not to use that word."

"Well, Paul, I say it the way I see it, and you should too! They are what they are. I have to go, but you know where I'll be. If you need me, call. And one more thing, Paul: I love you and I want you to stay safe." She gave me a hug that I thought would take my breath away or crack my ribs. Then she kissed me on my cheek and turned to walk out the front door. If I didn't know any better, I would have thought she had tears in her eyes. My mom very seldom cried.

Jerry got to my house soon after Mom left, but this time he wasn't his same old self. He didn't ring the front bell. He knocked gently on the back door. I looked out before I unlocked it, because I couldn't believe it was him. As I opened the door, as pleased as I was to see he had changed his ways, I had to ask him, "Why?"

He said, "I wanted to make sure no one was hiding behind the door." We didn't laugh at that though.

As he walked in, I saw a piece of pipe in his hand. "What's that for?"

"I wanted to be ready for anything," he said. And again there was no laugh. "I'm sorry, Paul, but I thought you were in trouble again. I thought they made you call me."

"No, I'm sorry, Jerry. My mom and dad were still home and I couldn't talk."

"Well, I guess I don't need this then." He laid the pipe on the kitchen table. "I don't know what I would have done with it anyway."

"Well, I know you sure did well with that fishing pole, Jerry."

"Yeah, I know! And that's why they want to kill me too, Paul! So you tell me, Paul, is violence good?

"What's on your mind, Paul?" He was still a little quiet for Jerry, but it didn't take long for him to get back to his old self after he'd heard my idea.

"I think we should organize a Saturday night campout at the park. You know, the last one before school starts." He looked at me with dagger eyes. "Is this so you don't have to climb out your window, Paul?" he asked.

"Well, yes, but if it works, we'll be closer to the Webster el, and we can get out and away easier. And if all goes well, we'll be back before we're missed."

"Yeah! Like the time we took off after the boys stoned your mom's car," Jerry said with a sneer.

"No, Jerry, this time we'll plan it. Have you still got that old tent, Jerry?"

"Yes, but I have that new one. It's bigger and it's lighter."

"No, we need that old one, because it's got zippers on both ends."

"Okay! I see," Jerry said. "That's a great idea. We can slip out and get back in without anyone seeing us. Okay!"

"Now," I said, "we have to get someone to chaperone us, and I'm sure we can get a bunch of the guys to go. They're always looking for something to do."

"Last time we did a campout, Jeff Chapel's dad took us. He loves cooking his chili outdoors and sitting by the fire and falling asleep," Jerry said."

"Yeah!" I said. "You want to call him?"

"Sure, his dad will be perfect."

The phone rang at Jeff's house about four times and we thought for sure no one would answer, but then Jeff picked up and said, "Yeah!"

"Jeff, this is Jerry."

"Hey, Jerry, don't you sleep? It's early yet."

"Sure, Jeff, but Paul and I are putting together an overnight campout at the park this Saturday. You want to come?"

Now that woke Jeff up. "Sure thing. My dad just bought a new tent."

"Can he be our cook?" Jeff asked.

"You know he loves to cook out."

"Yeah, that's right," Jerry said, "he makes that great chili over the fire. Well, we need an adult with us or we can't go. So if he doesn't mind."

I could hear Jeff on the phone yelling at his dad to pick up the phone, but his mom said he was outside. Jeff said, "I'll call you back in a few."

"Okay," Jerry said. "I'm at Paul's house. Have you got the number?"

I heard Jeff yell "sure," and then Jerry hung up.

While we waited for Jeff, we called some of the other guys. Almost all of them were ready for a campout. We had a few more to call, but Jeff called back and said his dad thought it was a great idea and said he'd be honored to be cook and chaperone. "By the way," Jeff said, "my dad just bought a bigger truck just for when we go camping. I guess he can try it out for this campout."

"Okay," Jerry said. "I'll let you know all the details tomorrow, including how many are going." Again I heard Jeff talking. I guess Jerry wasn't the loudest guy I knew. Jerry hung up the phone and looked at me. "Boy, that guy's a lot louder than me, Paul."

I wanted to tell him that I'd just been thinking the same thing and that I'd heard the whole conversation, but I said nothing. I just laughed.

"And Paul, that was a great idea, but like I heard my dad say the other day, he gets scared when things go too well."

"Yeah, I know what he means, but it beats falling out a second-floor window and getting caught by my mom and dad and having a broken leg while I'm trying to convince them I was sleepwalking." Jerry laughed, but I was dead serious as I turned and went into the kitchen.

My next big problem was whether or not Mom would let me go, but I couldn't worry about that just yet. We needed to plan our trip and our escape.

That night when Mom got home, she was in a good mood. She had gotten a raise at work and she was happier than I had seen her in a long time. I thought that it would be a good time to ask about a campout. And to my surprise, she didn't say no. "Well, you went on one last year," she said, "and it worked out well, so why not now? As long as your dad is fine with it and we get to talk to the chaperone."

"Well, you know Mr. Chapel, Jeff's dad, He's going to take us all to the park, like last year, and make his famous chili over the fire." As Mom and I talked, the phone rang. "I got it, Mom. It's probably one of the guys about the campout."

CHAPTER

17

Hero Works His Magic

To MY SURPRISE IT was Randolph calling. He told me to read today's newspaper. "Lower front page. I'm sure you all will be very interested. And I'll talk to you later," he said. "I am meeting with my friends tonight after work, about you and Black Dog. See you later, Paul. I've got to go." And he hung up.

"Mom!" I yelled. "Have we got today's paper?"

"Yes, it's still folded up on the kitchen counter, I just brought it in. Why?"

"I don't know, but Randolph just called and told me we should read it."

I opened the paper with a great deal of speed, almost ripping it. Mom told me to slow down or else we wouldn't be able to read it.

Another Black Dog story caught my eye. I laid the paper out on the table and started to read. Mom stood behind me.

The story read as follows:

> Throughout the years there have been numerous sightings of a large black dog helping people in distress and then disappearing as fast as he arrived. Well, once again late Sunday night, the large black dog appeared to work his magic, as most witnesses call it, when seventy-six-year old Martin Stork and his seventy-four-year old

wife Gail were on their way home from their grandson's birthday party, when their car was struck in the driver's side by another car, at the intersection of Webster and Sheffield. Mr. Stork's car was pushed sideways across the intersection and flipped over onto its roof, just before slamming into a light pole and catching on fire. Both occupants were unconscious in the burning car. Witnesses say the fire was too hot for them to get close enough to help, but they called police and the fire department.

Then, witnesses say, a large black dog came from nowhere, climbed halfway into the broken window of the burning car, pulled the woman out by her coat, and dragged her to safety before help got there. Then it went around to the other side of the burning car, went right back in, dragged the man out by his coat sleeve, and dragged him away from the burning car too.

When police and the fire department arrived, both occupants were still unconscious, and were transported to the hospital.

Police said that as they arrived at the scene of accident, they saw a very large black dog dragging a man across the street. The dog had smoke rising from its body, as though it had been burned, but it never stopped. The dog then stood looking around as if to see if others were going to help the two victims. It then looked back at the two people on the ground, and in a flash, it was gone.

Mr. and Mrs. Stork spent a few nights at the hospital and were released to their son for further home care, with minor cuts and burns. The other driver was unhurt.

> The reporter of this story and this Chicago newspaper would like to thank that big black dog for being the hero that it is, and its owners, whoever they might be, for the training it took to help these people in need.

Mom had tears in her eyes this time for sure, but she didn't try to hide them. I just looked at her and said nothing. After a while she said, "It sure makes me proud to know this dog is your friend, Paul."

"I know, Mom." She started putting dinner on the table, and this time I helped with no other reason except to help her.

It wasn't long before Dad came through the front door. But unlike his usual self, he had unlocked the door, slammed it open, and closed it hard, and stomped into the kitchen before we knew it.

It scared Mom half to death. She yelled out Jerry's name, believing for sure it was him.

"Have you seen the paper today?" Dad asked. He stood waving his paper at us.

"Yes," Mom said. I nodded. "We read that story about Black Dog, if that's what you mean." Dad was so excited that he seemed to take on some of my ways. Mom said, "Slow down, honey. You're going to have a heart attack."

"Well, I know, but this dog is like part of our family, and he made the front page of one of the biggest newspapers in the country again. But what I can't understand is why has no one ever seen this dog more than once, and that's when he's doing a good deed. He must live somewhere around this neighborhood, because all the stories we've read that Randolph left for us happened not far from here, including this one."

"Except me, Dad," I said, interrupting him.

"That's what I was going to say, Paul. He helped each of these people out of their tight spots just once, and as the newspaper stories go, they never saw him again, except you, Paul. He has some kind of tie with you."

"Randolph is meeting with some people tonight, honey," Mom said, "and he'll let us know whatever he finds out. He talked to Paul and told him about the newspaper story, so we'll just have to wait until he calls. Now let's eat."

Well, we didn't hear from Randolph that night, and maybe that was good. Mom had spent most of dinner telling Dad about her raise, and I quickly broke in with my camping trip. I wasn't sure Dad was listening to either of us. He just said, "That will be fun, Paul," without looking up. He just kept on eating. Mom looked at me and nodded as if to say, *Eat.* Dad sure was in another world with this Black Dog thing.

The next day was Friday. I needed sleep after being up early this morning. Jerry and I had a lot to do. Speak of the devil, just as I was going up to bed, Jerry called all excited about the story of Black Dog. "We read it, Jerry. Yes," I said, "it sounds like him. I don't know what to think right now, Jerry. But I'm tired and I'm going to bed. I'll see you here tomorrow. Bye."

CHAPTER 18

Making Plans

JERRY GOT TO THE house early, even before Mom and Dad left. Given the way he looked, I wondered if he'd even gone to bed. I was still in bed. He jumped on it and scared me to death. He was yelling something about Black Dog. "Jerry, I think you've been drinking your dad's beer, or something worse."

"You're nuts. Paul. Think about it. If Black Dog was out helping those people Sunday night, how could he be in a cage in the dummy's garage, or anywhere else as a matter of fact?"

"Well, you're right about that, Jerry, but if they had Jake's dad build that big cage for them, they must have something up their sleeves. And I bet it's not for raising dogs."

"Did you eat yet?" I asked.

"No! I was too excited," Jerry said. "I wanted to get over here and plan for tomorrow."

"Yeah, me too. But I'm going to eat a big breakfast, Jerry, because it might be the last one I ever get."

"Now that's not funny, Paul," Jerry said. He left my room and went downstairs.

I answered with, "I know. It wasn't meant to be."

I heard Mom yell up that she was leaving. I just yelled, "Okay, Mom!" I got dressed and went downstairs to find Jerry on the phone, talking to someone about the campout.

"That was Mike Little. He's going too. That was the last of them. That makes eleven guys going camping."

"While you make breakfast, I'll make a list. I talked to Jeff this morning, and his dad wants it with everyone's name and phone number, in case he needs to call a parent for some reason."

A little after 10:00 a.m. the phone rang. Jerry and I were sitting outside. Both of us jumped up and ran inside, and almost ran into each other. Jerry grabbed the phone and said, "Hello!" Then stood listening to the voice on the other end. He tried to talk but couldn't get a word out of his mouth. This time I couldn't hear the voice, but I saw Jerry trying to speak. Again he couldn't say a thing. Then he said, "Yes, okay!" and hung up.

"Who was that, Jerry?"

"Well, I would have given you the phone, but he just kept talking and I couldn't say anything."

"Well, who was it?" I said with my stern voice.

"It was Randolph."

"Randolph? What did he want?"

"Well, he was talking so fast that I really couldn't understand him. But this I do know: he asked if we were going to be here for a while and said that he was coming over, and I said, 'Yes, okay!' And then he hung up. I think he was saying something about he knows the secret to Black Dog."

I called Grandpa and told him to come over. Mom would have a fit if we didn't get the story straight, and she would believe him before she'd believed me about anything to do with Black Dog.

Jerry and I sat outside waiting for Randolph and Grandpa to arrive. Everything was running through my head now. Could Marvin and Jake really catch Black Dog and cage him somehow? Or could it be possible that I was walking into a trap to help Black Dog and bringing Jerry with me? What if there wasn't any Black Dog around to help us. After all, I hadn't seen him in a long time. Also there were times when the boys had showed up and there was no Black Dog. I sure wished I knew where he was right now and if he was okay. That car accident happened last Saturday night, and this was Friday. The police said his hair was smoking as if he had been burned. He might have been burned bad enough to die, or maybe he needed help. I wish I knew. One thing I did know for sure: it was my turn to help him.

It wasn't long before Grandpa got there, and soon after Randolph pulled up in a very hurried manner, as Mario called it when he was dealing with Jerry.

Randolph was out of the car and standing in front of us before we could wave hello. He greeted Grandpa. Jerry and I stood staring at him, waiting for him to speak to us. "How about the kitchen table, Paul? We need to talk." Grandpa nodded a yes as I looked at him for an answer.

"Well, Paul," Randolph said, "I find it hard to tell stories that I can't prove, but I told you guys that I'd look into this Black Dog story. And that's why I'm here. But before I say any more, I have questions for you.

"First of all, start at the very beginning, you know, where you first saw Black Dog?"

'That's easy," I said. "I was with Mom at Mario's store." I told the whole story as they all looked on, never saying a word. I told them about him taking the meat and lying down and eating it, and how I had to go to the bathroom, so I closed my eyes and wished I was in the bathroom, and when I opened them he was gone.

"Were you scared of him?" Randolph asked.

"I was too scared to move, because he was so big. Then I decided to open my eyes and go for it. But like I said, he was gone, like he was reading my mind."

"Good, Paul. When was the very next time you saw Black Dog?"

"Well, when I tried to outsmart Marvin and the boys by going home another way."

Randolph and the others looked at me and nodded their heads. "Wait a minute, Paul, was this the first time you had trouble with the boys?"

"No, sir, that all started a long time ago in school. But they chased me a few other times after school, and I think because there were other people around they gave up, or maybe they just got meaner since then. I used to go home different ways and they never found me. It started to be a game with me, just to see if I could beat them at their own game.

But there were only four of them, whereas now there are five. Barry just came to our school this year and joined their gang.

"That's how I met Mario. They chased me into an alley, all five of them, but I got away when I hit Jake in the chest with my book bag. And then I threw my book bag at Barry and got him in the leg. They both went down. I ran as fast as I could down to the alley by Mario's store. I hid behind some dumpsters till they were gone. They saw Mario come out, and they took off after throwing my school bag in a dumpster. You know what's really funny? That's the same dumpster that Black Dog made Jake get in to get away from him when they threw rocks at Mom's car."

"Well, that tells us why they hate you, doesn't it?" Randolph said. "A fifth grader did all this to them and there was only one of you and five of them. They sure don't want the whole school to know that they all lost to one fifth grader and a dog, a dog that they couldn't even prove was really there."

Grandpa said, "It sure sounds like you can take care of yourself, Paul."

"It all happened so fast that I just did what I could without thinking."

"Go on, Paul," Randolph said.

"Well, I left school one day, like I said, and tried to outsmart them by going a really long way home. But they found me as I walked down this quiet street. I knew I was in big trouble because there were no people and not many cars. By the way, that's the first time I saw the old bearded man with that walking stick. He was tapping it on the concrete as he walked. I could hear him a long way down the street. Then I heard the boys calling me names, and there they were. Marvin picked me up and threw me on the ground." Grandpa's face turned beet red as I told that story.

"Paul," Randolph said, "were you scared?" I looked at Jerry and Grandpa and then down at the table. I said, "I was more scared that day than ever before in my life. I knew I had more trouble than I could ever believe. I also knew then that I should have told someone.

"I hit Jake with that bag. And I knew it would not be over until he killed me or hurt me real bad. I guess I wished real hard to have a big, mean friend who could help me just this one time so I could get home and tell someone all about the bullies, because that's just what I got, a big, mean friend.

"First Marvin threw me on the ground after they took my book bag. The tears were rolling down my cheeks. Then they were going to take turns beating me up. Jake was going to be first. He picked me up like a bag of rags and spun me around. Then from nowhere, Black Dog appeared. Marvin asked me if he was mine. As I turned, I could see Black Dog looked ready to kill, and we all thought he would, including me. I said, 'Yes, I guess he is.' They said they had just been joking with me and asked if they could leave. I said yes, but it was as if Black Dog was reading my mind again. They still had my book bag. I started to say something, but Black Dog let out a sound that stopped us all. 'My bag,' I said. They gave it back, and Black Dog let them go. He stayed until they were out of sight, and then he was gone. All the way home I looked for him and the bullies, but I never saw any of them."

"Go on, Paul," Randolph said, writing in a notebook.

"I sure didn't want to tell about them coming in my house after me, at least not in front of Grandpa, but I did. I'm sorry, Grandpa. I never wanted to lie to you, but at the time I had to for Black Dog's sake. I told them about the park and how Jerry and I fought them off with our fishing poles and how they ran away a little bloody. And Jerry noticed his hook and sinker were missing. We didn't laugh at that though. We figured the hook was still in Jake's hand." Grandpa and Randolph really got a kick out of that one.

"Were you scared at the park, Paul?" Randolph asked.

"Not like when I was out on the street alone. I had Jerry with me. And there were people out there."

"And you didn't see Black Dog at all that day?"

"No. Marvin and Jake were looking for him and asked me where my brother dog was. That's when Jake went after me and said he was going to throw me in the lagoon. Then Jerry went after them with the pole, and I followed. And they took off. You know they had Barry steal my bike this summer, and Black Dog got it back at the park?"

"Yes, I heard that. And did you get scared when you found your bike missing?"

"Well, yes. I knew I was supposed to keep it locked at all times."

"This may seem like a strange question to you all, but I was told to ask you to give me a number from one to ten, one being not so scared and ten being the worst, when you found your bike missing."

I had to think about that one for a moment. As I did so, Grandpa said, "Do you understand that question, Paul?"

"Yes, but I think at first it was like a three or four, because I thought someone was just playing a joke on me. Then as I got closer to the house, it became an eight. My dad doesn't get mad often, so I wasn't sure how mad he would be now, but I did know he wasn't going to be happy to see me coming home without my bike."

"Well, from what I know now about Black Dog, and if you all think about it, he only shows up when you're really scared. I mean, really scared. Like number seven or more.

"Let me ask you something else, Paul—and think about this before you answer."

"Sure," I said.

"When your mom's car got hit by the rocks and she crashed, were you scared then?"

"You know, I wasn't scared that night by the crash, I think because it happened so fast. I think I was mad. Because I got out of the front seat to see if Grandma was okay, and that's when I saw the boys take off."

"How mad were you, Paul?"

"Probably ten on your scale, Randolph." That made everyone laugh, including me.

"Well, last night I spent my time after work with a bunch of people who have been following these Black Dog stories for years, and they gave me a lot of insight on why he has picked you to watch over. I have all I need right now," Randolph said.

The phone rang. I let Jerry answer it. "I'll call you back" we heard him say. Then he said, "Eleven plus your dad. Okay! Bye.

"It was Jeff. He just wanted to know how many were going camping tomorrow." Grandpa's eyes lit up at the word *camping*. We all looked at him and waited for him to speak.

"Do you think this is a good idea, Paul? I mean with these guys out to get you?"

"Well, Grandpa, I can't hide in the house the rest of my life. Besides, have you ever seen Jeff Chapel's dad, Grandpa?"

"No, Paul, I don't think so."

"Well, he's a bodybuilder and about six foot six, and he loves the outdoors. He always tells us that if he could get his wife to move, he would live in the mountains in a log cabin and catch his food."

"Oh, yes, Paul," Grandpa said, "I did meet him. I met him here at a party your mom and dad had last year. Yes, he is big—and very hard to forget."

"Well, Grandpa, he's the one taking all of us camping, and he's a great cook."

"Well, okay, Paul, but watch your back."

"I will. And thanks, Grandpa."

Randolph excused himself. "Time for work," he said, "but I'd rather be camping with you guys."

"You can come if you want," Jerry said. I tried not to show my anger as he spoke, but you can bet I'd give it to him later.

"No thanks, Jerry. I have to work Saturday, and then I have a date." We all laughed. "What? You don't think that's possible? I'm no bodybuilder, but I sure can dance. See you all later," he said.

We went out the front door and watched him as he drove away. Then Grandpa said his goodbyes and left. As he got in his car, he pointed his finger at Jerry and me and said, "Remember, boys, watch your backs." Then he drove off.

"Jerry," I said, as I gave him a shove away from me, "what's wrong with you?"

"What Paul?"

"The more people watching us, the harder it'll be to sneak away."

"Oh yeah!" he said. "I didn't think of that. Sorry!"

CHAPTER

Going Camping 19

Early Saturday morning all the guys started showing up at my house, unloading tents, fishing poles, and everything else they needed for the campout from their parents' cars. Mom made a lot of food the night before, and so did the other moms. I think we had enough food for a week. Jeff, his dad, and his dad's white German shepherd named Lady, who had a most unusual collar, showed up about ten with the big new truck and a lot more food. Jerry gave the list of names and phone numbers to Jeff after we loaded everything onto the truck. We settled down in the back while Mr. Chapel talked to Mom and Dad and a few of the other boys' parents. Then Jeff's dad gave us the rundown on how to ride in the back of the truck. You could tell he meant just what he said: "Arms in, and sit at all times, understand?" Mom and Dad stood watching as he spoke.

We all answered, "Yes, sir."

"Jeff, you know the rules in the truck better than anyone, so you're in charge out here." You could see Mom's and Dad's faces light up, like they knew we were in good hands. We all waved goodbye. Mr. Chapel's dog Lady got to ride shotgun, while Jeff took on his responsibility of being the boss in the back.

"Hey, Jeff," I said, "why does your dog's collar have that bell on it?"

"Well," Jeff said as he laughed a little, "she likes to hunt when we go out of town camping. Which is okay. But when she catches things, she likes to eat them too! That's not good. Rabies come from animals, so the bell makes just enough noise to scare whatever she's hunting away. But she sure gets a lot of exercise trying to find things to eat."

It wasn't far to the park, but we had to stop and get bait and firewood. I think we waved at everyone we saw, after we'd asked Jeff if his dad would get mad. Jeff said, "No, just keep your hands inside the truck."

This would have been a great way to end the summer, if I didn't have to worry about tonight. If I could have thought of another way to save Black Dog, I'm sure I would have. I knew that if I told anyone, the cops would be there looking for the bullies, and Marvin would hurt Black Dog, just to prove he could.

We all set up our tents and helped get the food ready for lunch. Jerry and I set up his tent with its back to the lagoon so we could get out without being seen by anyone.

"You know, Paul," Jerry said, "we have to watch out for the horse patrol. They're all over this park at night."

"You're right, Jerry. And the cops on those horses all look like they're as big as Jeff's dad."

"Also, Paul, if we're seen on the street by the police at all late at night, we're dead.

"Well, Jerry, we'll just have to start thinking like Marvin and the boys. They always get away with it. They're out all night long stealing stuff."

"I asked Barry about how they did that, Paul, and he said, 'It's easy. We don't use the streets. We use the alleys and gangways all the time.' Do you know how to be like Marvin and the boys, Paul?"

"Well, I know a little more now, and maybe that's why they wear those dirty black clothes. No one can see them at night."

"Sorry, Paul, I didn't bring any dirty black clothes with me."

"That's funny," I said. We laughed our way over to the fire. "Try to borrow what you can from the other guys. Tell them you need the clothes to fish tonight, that you forgot yours at home. But make sure they're black, although they don't have to be dirty, Jerry. Tell them that it keeps the bugs away. I'm going to check my things. I think my mom packed my black jacket. She always packs much more than I need."

"You think she's trying to tell you something, Paul? Like, don't come home to soon?"

"Maybe, Jerry. I never thought of that. I'll have to talk to her when I get home."

"With all those clothes and all that food she made, I'd give it some thought," he said.

"We're making jokes right now. Let's see how much we laugh tonight," I said.

"Thanks for destroying the mood again, Paul."

This time I said, "I'm sorry. Let's eat lunch."

It wasn't long before everyone settled into some daytime fishing or a good game of ball. After a while, Jerry and I made our way over to the fire to figure out how we would get out of here without getting caught. "We have to stuff our beds to make them look slept in. Did you get black clothes?"

"Yeah," Jerry said. "I had black pants. I guess my mom is like yours. And I borrowed a black jacket. What about you?"

"I have both," I said. "My mom says black is easy to get clean."

Mr. Chapel came over to the fire to check the chili. "You boys don't want to play ball?"

"We did for a while. But we wanted to sit and watch the fire and see the sun set," I said.

"Yeah!" Jerry said. "And smell the chili."

"Well, it's ready to eat, so if you two want to collect the others, we'll eat. I'll get the bread and the bowls, and you can tell everyone to wash up."

We all sat around the fire on the ground, ready to eat. But first Mr. Chapel had us join hands just like at lunchtime. Then he thanked the Lord for the food and our good health. He added, "Lord, can you watch over these boys in their growing times and help them make the right decisions, and help them wake up every day of their lives with smiles on their faces? Amen, let's eat," he said.

I guess I was thinking about what he'd said about making the right decisions, knowing that no matter how this turned out, what we were doing was wrong. But Black Dog was out there and I needed to find him.

After we all helped clean up, we sat around the fire just talking, telling jokes, having a great time, and watching the sun set. Before I knew it, it was after nine and half the guys had gone to bed. We helped Mr. Chapel put more wood on the fire and clean up and get ready for breakfast. Then I said good night and made my way over to the tent. Jerry had gone to sleep earlier, having told me to wake him when I was ready to go. I sure gave that some thought. *It might be better for us if I just leave without him.* But that thought didn't last long. He was awake when I crawled into the tent.

"Hey, Paul, did you think I'd let you off that easy?"

"What do you mean, Jerry?"

"You know what I mean: leave without me. You thought I'd fall asleep. Well, first of all, Paul, you always fall asleep first, and second, you sleep through a storm and I awake at the drop of a pin. So you're stuck with me."

I said nothing. I just lay down and closed my eyes. I was scared, but I wasn't about to tell anyone.

"Paul, I'm no sissy, and you know I'd do anything for you and Black Dog, but you have to admit, we're crazy for what we are about to do. This is big trouble, and the people around us won't forget easily. There's five or more of them and only two of us. Maybe we could get at least a few of the other guys to go too."

"First off, Jerry, it's too late. And second of all, someone would tell. Then where would Black Dog be? No, Jerry, no help. I'm going alone if I have to. And you know that."

"Well, I'm going with you, and you know that."

"Okay! In a little while, Jerry. I just want to lie here and think about our next move."

It wasn't long before I jumped to my feet and almost knocked the whole tent down on top of us. Jerry wasn't sleeping, but I guessed I'd dozed off. "Paul!" he said quietly, "sit down. You're too tall to stand in this old tent." He grabbed my arm and pulled me down. "And be quiet or you'll have all of Chicago hearing you."

"What time is it?" I asked.

"It's ten to ten."

"We better make these beds look like we're sleeping in them," I said. "That's why I brought theses extra blankets."

"I thought you brought them to snuggle up next to, because your mommy isn't here."

"Funny, Jerry."

I peeked out the front of the tent and looked around. "I think everyone is asleep."

"Yeah. Mr. Chapel checked on us with his dog a little while ago. I heard the zipper go up, and then he looked in. I didn't say anything, but his dog came halfway in and backed out. I'm surprised you didn't hear her bell. And then he zipped the zipper down and moved on."

"Okay! The beds look good. Now, black clothes and we are out of here. And bring your flashlight. Put it in your pocket, but don't use it unless you really have to. We don't want to show anyone where we are.

"Are you ready, Jerry?"

"Ready as I'm ever going to be," he whispered.

"Yeah, me too! Let's go." I unzipped the rear of the tent slowly. I knew Lady was sleeping out in front of Mr. Chapel's tent, just across the fire pit. Even if she didn't bark, the sound of that bell as she moved around would attract attention. I reminded Jerry about her, and we crawled out quietly. I pulled the zipper back down. As we moved slowly away from the campsite, the fire with fresh wood burning on it made enough noise to cover up our movement.

CHAPTER 20 Chicago, Big and Scary

I REALIZED ONCE AGAIN that I was only eleven years old and I was taking on much more than I wanted to. The city was big and, as I said before, scary. Now I found out that to stay out of sight, I had to dress as my hunters did, and travel the same routes my hunters used. That's why they always found me while I was running from them, because I was using their alleys, which they knew better than I did. The day I hit them with my book bag and ran, they didn't run. They didn't have to. They knew where I would go.

Jerry led the way. We headed across the park to the city streets and the alleys, over to the Webster Street el. It was almost too quiet there to be a city as big as Chicago. Every little sound made the hair stand up on the back of my neck.

We made our way over to Lincoln Avenue, staying out of the reach of most people. We spotted two cops on horseback at the edge of the park, and quickly hid long enough for them to go by as they talked. They never saw us. The people who did see us just passed us by like we were not there. That's when I started to find out that what my parents said about people is true. They don't want to get involved. They didn't even make eye contact.

We hit Lincoln Avenue, but there was too much life out there for two eleven-year-old boys to be out that late at night, including police in cars and a few walking their beats. We had to hide a few times to escape being caught.

Jerry and I talked it over. He knew more about this area more than I did, so he led the way. After we turned off Lincoln Avenue and onto a side street, we headed one block over to the alley that ran behind Lincoln Avenue. It was like heading into hell. I could only think of a movie I saw at the Biograph Theater not long ago about a deep dark dungeon loaded with dead people and everything bad that you could think of. That was the first and last of dungeon movies for me.

I was hoping it was my imagination, but I was almost sure that the sounds I kept hearing were coming from the garbage cans. I stopped Jerry and said, "Listen, do you hear that?"

"Yes, Paul, I hear it. And that's why I'm not stopping. Let's go. It's almost 10:30."

As we got to the next side street, we ran into three young men smoking in front of an apartment building. "What are you boys doing out here this late?" one of them asked.

"Looking for my dog that got out of the house a little while ago," I answered quickly. "And when my mom and dad get home, they're goanna be real mad."

"What's your dog look like, kid?" the biggest one asked.

"He's big and black and looks like a bear."

"Well, boys, it's strange, but we've been out here about forty-five minutes since we got home from work and we haven't seen that big black dog of yours—"

And Jerry, as Jerry is prone to doing, cut him off. "Well, thank you anyway. We have to go," Jerry said to them, grabbing my arm and giving me a tug. "You know, find our dog."

Then the big guy said, "But what is strange, as I started to say, is as long as we've lived here and stood out here after work, we have never seen as many dogs go by as we've seen tonight." The other two guys agreed. "There must have been fifty dogs come out of that alley and from each far end of the street. I think you'll find your dog down there somewhere. They were all headed in the same direction, and that's real weird." As he spoke, he pointed down the alley, the same way we were headed. "Hey! Before you go," the big guy said, "you need to change your looks a little." He started to step forward, but then he stopped quickly.

"Okay, little guy," he said as he held up his hands, "I just wanted to help."

I had no idea what was going on until I turned to see Jerry, who all this time had been behind me. He stood stiff as a pole, with his hands held high in the air, holding a piece of pipe and ready to do battle with this big guy. "What do you mean, change our looks?" Jerry yelled.

"Well," the guy said. "if you're catching a family dog or just getting out for some fresh air like us at this time of night in Chicago, you better look like you can take care of yourself."

"Yeah!" Jerry said, still holding the pipe high.

"Well, lift your collar like this," he said, pulling up on his own. Me, I followed and did the same, but not Jerry; he just stood silent. "And, boys, the big guy said, "you need to mess up your hair a little. You look too much like this is your first time on your own in the nightlife."

Wonder what gave him that idea? I thought to myself. The other two guys agreed, so I messed up my hair, and then I reached over and rubbed Jerry's head. We all laughed. Jerry lowered the pipe, tucked it into the back of his belt, and pulled his black jacket down over it. He grabbed his collar and pulled it up, and then he looked up at the big guy and smiled. I thanked them, and we left.

"Boy, oh boy, Jerry, we learn something new every day."

"Yeah, Paul! My dad calls it street training."

"What's going on down here with these dogs, Jerry?"

"There are a lot of restaurants, Paul, that are open late. Maybe someone cleaned out their refrigerator and the dogs got the scent. It's 10:45. We have three blocks to go. We lost too much time hiding from cops and not walking," Jerry said.

As we walked, I talked. "We want to see Marvin and Jake before they see us. And I don't want them to know you're with me."

"Why, Paul?"

"Because you may need to go for help while they're beating me up."

"That's not funny, Paul."

"I'm not trying to be funny this time. When we find them, we'll split up and just watch and see where they go. After I don't show, they may leave and lead us to Black Dog. If they do, you can go for help and I'll stay near them but out of sight."

"Well, Paul, that's the el two streets up, but this alley ends one block before we get there, because of the el. And it's all fenced. We should go to the end of the alley, go right, cross Webster Avenue, and find them while we're still together."

"Jerry! Look at those dogs running down the alley."

"Yeah! I saw them. They just came out of that gangway, Paul."

Mario had told me about stray dog packs and how they roamed the alleys looking for food.

"I heard that they're not all strays, Paul. Some people let their dogs out at night to find food so the owners don't have to buy as much."

"That's mean, Jerry."

"Yeah! Well, what about the people who send their kids out to do the same thing? Maybe that's why Marvin and his boys steal food from wherever they can get it, Jerry! Those dogs went right to the end of the alley. I don't want to run into them, so we should both go left and see where it takes us."

"We can't do that, Paul. We have to take our chances with the dogs and hope they're gone. We have to get out that way to Webster Avenue before Marvin and them think you're not coming and they leave. It's almost 11:00 now. I doubt if they'll be standing out where we can see them. They sure don't want the police to see them."

"Yeah, you're right, Jerry."

"Okay! Here we are, Paul. We have to go up this side street just a little way and back to Webster, but before we cross, we need to look around to see if they're out there. We don't know what side of the street they're on, so we should cross the street and go down a little ways and then come in from the back of the pizza place."

"Okay, Jerry, but tell me this: Do you think you could use that pipe on them?"

"No, and I don't want to hurt anyone. You know that. It's not like a fishing pole. A piece of pipe could kill. But it's always good to be prepared.

"Yeah, I guess. Oh, by the way, Paul, this one's yours," he said as he lifted his jacket.

"What?" I yelled.

He handed me a pipe, and said, "I didn't give it to you before because I knew you wouldn't like it. But these aren't regular schoolkids we're dealing with. I have an older sister who has older boyfriends who talk a lot when I'm around, and I listen. I remember one of them saying to his friend, 'Cops carry guns, but they don't shoot unless they have to. And they hardly ever have to because people know they will when things call for it.' You can bet your life on this, Paul: the bullies won't come empty-handed."

"Jerry, over there! Do you see those dogs eating that garbage?"

"Yes, Paul, but we have to go by them. Stay to the right, Jerry, away from them. Maybe we'll be okay. They're small dogs, and there's only three that I can see."

As we passed the dogs eating their dinner from a knocked-over garbage can, they stopped to look at us. Then like we weren't even there, they went back to their dinner.

"Okay, Paul, it's time to cross the street."

"Wait, Jerry, that's Sammy over by the front door of the pizza place. You see him? He's standing behind those two men."

"Yeah, now I see him. Maybe he's with them," Jerry said.

"No, I think he's standing there to make the police think he's with them."

"I wonder where the others are hiding," Jerry said.

"I bet they're not far away," I said, "just waiting to take my head off." My heart started pounding at the sight of Sammy. I could feel my knees getting weaker, just like the time in the street. I knew it was the fear of death or injury that I was feeling. If Randolph asked me now for a number, if would be somewhere around twenty. "Let's just stay here awhile and see where he goes," I said.

"Okay! We should know something soon," Jerry said. "It's after eleven. Here comes some more of those dogs behind us. Looks like five or six this time."

"Yeah, Jerry, and they're a lot bigger than the last few we saw. They don't look too friendly either."

Jerry said, "Maybe we should go now, before they get an idea we're their dinner."

"No. If we move, we won't be able to see Sammy. I think if we ignore the dogs, they'll just leave us alone. After all, we're not that smelly. We just took showers this morning. Dogs like their food to smell bad."

"I hope you're right," Jerry said. "You see that one closest to us, the biggest one? He has a limp, and from what I can see from the light on that pole there, he has one eye missing. And he doesn't look friendly."

Just before the dogs got to us, we all heard a loud bark from somewhere in the distance. I looked at Jerry and smiled. they turned and headed the other way, toward the sound. We weren't sure why, but we were glad. All the time we talked, we kept an eye on Sammy. After a while, he moved to the side of the pizza place and stood there, under the el. As we watched him doing nothing, I had time to think about when I was younger and feared the el because of all the noise it made and because it showered sparks down on us as it flew by. Mom told me then that it was just a train like other trains but that it was built up in the air on steel beams so it could go faster and not worry about traffic. That's why they call it the el. She said, "That's short for 'elevated train.'" It's funny when you see one go by and you're outside, like we were now, standing by the Webster Avenue el, how much noise it makes. It hurts your ears enough to make you cover them, but when you're inside one, it's quiet and smooth.

"Paul! There's Hank."

"Well, I'm betting the others are close behind," I said.

"Yeah! Let's hope so. This jacket might make me look tough with the collar pulled up, but it's not that warm. I'd like to be asleep in the tent, under all those blankets you brought."

"Oh, now you want to snuggle with my blankets because your mommy's not here."

"You got me back, Paul. Good one!"

He was right. The days were getting shorter and the nights getting colder.

We waited awhile longer, and then it happened. Sammy and Hank disappeared under the el after crossing Webster Avenue, over to our side. Now we had to follow them. At least we didn't have to cross the street to the side lit up by the pizza place, but we had to take a chance of being seen by Marvin and Jake. We knew they were somewhere close, but where?

"Jerry, do you think they'd head out to the train yard after getting caught stealing out there?"

"Knowing them," he said, "yes. That cage was made to take apart, Paul. They could have moved it anywhere."

"Well, time to go, Jerry, before they get too far ahead."

"Yeah, I guess."

We made our way over to the el structure and hid behind the steel beams. There wasn't much light under there, which was good, but it was also bad. We wanted to see them, but we didn't want them to see us.

"Jerry, we have to split up. You take this side, and I'm going over to the other side. This way, if they catch one of us, the other can go for help. But whatever you do, be very quiet. We need to follow them to find Black Dog. We're not here to get beat up by all of them."

"Okay, Paul, but you need to remember, Black Dog may not be anywhere around. So this fight might be ours and only ours if we do get caught."

"Yeah, I know, Jerry. Let's try to stay right across from each other. And good luck."

"You too, Paul," Jerry said as he put his hand out to shake my hand. That made me think about what friendship was all about, as I felt myself getting a little overwhelmed.

We followed like pros. Jerry went ahead and stopped, and then I took the lead for a while on my side. We went back and forth as we kept Sammy and Little Hank in sight. We saw more dogs off and on as we tailed them. Most stayed far enough away, and I was glad of that, but I knew none of them were Black Dog. If they had him or not, I wanted to know for sure. I knew being out here tonight was going to change my life forever, so no matter what happened out there, I would have to tell my story and end it. One way or the other, the bullies would be dealt with once this night is over, and Jerry and I would have to pay a price too. I was hoping the Almighty really did look out after foolish kids as Jeff's dad had asked the Lord to do.

We headed down about six more blocks under the el. I knew we were getting too close, because I could hear the boys talking. Jerry was up front on his side of the tracks. I had to get his attention, but I couldn't yell, so out came that heavy flashlight I'd carried in my pocket all night. Sammy stopped and turned around. He must have heard something. Hank, still walking, said, "Let's go. They're waiting for us."

"I heard something," Sammy said.

"Yeah! Some of those dogs looking to chew on you," Hank said. "And if I were you, I wouldn't stand in one place too long. Whatever the dogs leave, the rats finish off." He laughed, and they moved on.

Jerry waited for me to get up to where he was. Then he crossed over to my side, as Sammy and Hank moved ahead. "Did you hear what Hank said about 'they're waiting'?"

"Yeah! I heard. That's good, Jerry. At least we know they're not behind us." We stayed together this time as we moved from beam to beam. A train moved along the tracks above us, shooting sparks down to the ground, lighting up the whole area. Jerry and I hit the ground so we wouldn't be seen. We covered our ears. Then we stood up and moved ahead a little farther. Soon I put my hand up as if to say stop. Jerry looked at me. I pointed ahead of us to show him they'd stopped and were looking up at the top of a building. We moved behind an old car that looked like it had been there for years. Again, I started to wish I wasn't out there.

"Jerry, didn't Mary say she heard Jake saying they were going to rob a store?"

"Yeah, Paul."

We stayed kneeling down and waited to see what was next. "What time is it, Jerry?"

"Hang on, Paul. I think someone's on that roof, but I can't tell who it is. He threw a rope over the edge. Sammy's got the end. And there goes Hank, up to the roof. Sammy's going up now."

We watched him struggle halfway up the dangling rope. Then we heard him yelling, "Pull me up! Pull me up!" Then came a loud scream that should have been heard for miles as Sammy fell to the ground with more than a thud.

"Holy mackerel, Jerry, did you see that?"

"I did, Paul, and I loved it. I wish I had a camera." Thank God a train went over, because we couldn't hold in the laughter. As the train passed and the sparks flew, we could see very clearly that it was Marvin on the roof. He was looking over the side and yelling at Sammy to quit fooling around and get up there. Sammy tried to climb the rope, but he was hurt and couldn't do it. Then Jake popped his head over the side and told him to stay down there and just hold the rope when they come down.

It wasn't long before we heard voices from up top. "Grab this stuff when I send it down," Jake said. He had another rope he lowered down. It had a hook on it, and something was hanging from that hook.

Jerry and I moved to the front of the old car, where we could see better. "What kind of store is that, Jerry?" I asked.

"I have no idea, Paul. I don't know this part of town that well. But I do know this much: there is no Black Dog here. Not with them or with us. They lied about having Black Dog to get you here, and they figured I'd be here too. They wanted to beat us up under the el so no one could hear them do bodily harm to us. Now, Paul, I think it's about time we get back before we're noticed and Mr. Chapel uses that list to call our parents. Which might be better than him finding us."

"What time is it?"

"About eleven twenty, Paul."

"Okay, let's wait and see where they go with that stuff. They might have Black Dog there."

"Yeah, Paul! I thought you'd say that."

They lowered down a lot more things and climbed down themselves.

"They can't carry all that stuff, Paul. How are they going to move it?"

"Did you notice Barry isn't with them?" I said.

"Yeah that's what I mean. That's a lot of stuff for four guys to carry."

"Jerry! Jake's leaving."

"Yeah, I see that, Paul. Let's just stay right here and watch."

CHAPTER

21 Captured

ABOUT FIFTEEN MINUTES WENT by. I had to pee. "I'm going to the rear of the car, Jerry."

"Okay, I'll watch them." Jerry crawled to the rear of the car just as I finished. "Paul, get down under the car," he whispered. "Marvin's heading this way with Hank." We slid under that old car, into the bugs and the grime and the oil smell, and now the fresh pee, hoping we weren't sliding into a rats' nest. It almost made Jerry sick. He was gagging, but he held back.

We heard Marvin talking to Hank, and then we heard Jake's voice. "Hey, dog boy, do you want to come out with your other brother there, or do we pull you out?" We said nothing. "Okay, boys, last chance." Then someone reached under the car and grabbed my foot and started to pull. Whoever it was wasn't very pleasant about it. As he yanked me out, he turned my leg one way and then the other. It felt like it was being ripped off.

I heard Marvin yell, "Hey! Easy, Jake. We need those legs to carry our stuff. You can have him when we're done. Matter of fact Jake, you can have him and his dog. Won't that satisfy your urge?"

Jake said nothing. He just pulled me a little further than he had to, through the dirt, gravel, and garbage. As I lay there on my belly, I raised my head to see them pull Jerry out next. Now the Jerry I knew would have done something stupid to get them real mad. But he didn't even say a word. He just got right up and brushed himself off like he was playing a game of ball. Then I did the same.

As I stood up and turned to look at Jake, I saw Barry standing about twenty feet away from us. Then I looked back at Jerry. "He's there," Marvin said, "so don't think of running. That wouldn't be a good idea anyway if you ever want to see that dog of yours again." Marvin told Jerry and me to follow him, as he walked back to the store they'd just robbed. The sound of dogs barking seemed to overtake the area, but there were no dogs in sight. We all stopped to listen, even Marvin and Jake.

Jake grabbed Marvin by the arm and said, "These dogs are watching us."

"Don't be stupid, Jake," Marvin said. "They're no different than any other time we're out here."

"Then why did you stop when they barked if there are the same as any other time?" Jake asked Marvin.

Marvin looked at Jake, shaking his head, and said, "Let's go," with that look he always gave indicating *I'm the boss.*

Jake had lost his tough attitude. My thought was that since the time Black Dog had stripped their clothes from them in the alley, Jake's fear of dogs had become overwhelming. "We're going to move this stuff, and if you do what you're supposed to, we might not get nasty," Marvin told Jerry and me.

"Hey, Marvin!" I said. "Why should we help when you just told Jake he could have me and the dog?"

"Because, kid, you have no choice, just like I knew you had no choice when we had that girl put that note on your bike. You had to come for the dog's sake. Now let's get out of here." We all carried boxes and what seemed to be duffel bags and suitcases that were very heavy. Sammy must have been hurt bad from the fall, because he lagged far behind. At one time Marvin looked back at him and yelled, "Let's go." We all looked back to find him down on his knees and holding his chest. He got up on one knee, but he couldn't pick up the things he was carrying, so Barry, who was told to bring up the rear, gently helped him up the rest of the way and carried his things while Sammy also hung onto him.

We hadn't gotten far from the el when we cut through a gangway. I thought we were taking a shortcut to an alley, but Marvin stopped next to an old garage and put down his haul. He reached in his pocket and pulled out a single key. A small light barely glowed over the old garage door. "Marvin!" I said. "Why did you go through the roof to rob that store and not the front or rear door?"

"Because I have a friend who lives in the apartment next door. He lets us party there, and it was easier to go off his roof than trying to get through the steel front and rear doors."

Marvin dropped the key and went down to search for it in the tall grass and garbage. He couldn't find it, so he started swearing and kicking the door. I pulled the flashlight from my back pocket, which was still covered by my jacket. I shined it down on the ground and moved it around. It wasn't because I wanted to help Marvin, not by any means, but because I wanted to find Black Dog and go back to the park before they found us missing. If I … lived … long enough. Marvin took the light from me, but to my surprise he was gentle. He found the key and handed me back the light, which was another surprise. He unlocked the door and turned on a much brighter light inside. We all were told to carry in the stuff. And we did just that.

Jerry stood next to me inside the garage. He asked Marvin, "Where is Black Dog?"

"He's not here, but we have him. And now that you helped us rob that television store, maybe we can all be better friends." I looked at Jerry as he reached behind his back very slowly. I shook my head no at him, and his arm came back empty. Marvin and Jake started to laugh, but Sammy was in no laughing mood. He was leaning on an old table in pain. Barry stood next to him. Hank stood by the door so we couldn't get out.

"Okay then, what's next?" I said.

"Well, we go get the dog."

"Where is he?"

"Not far. But don't try running, because, like I said before, we don't have to chase you. We will just kill your dog, and you'd still have to prove you didn't help us rob that store. It's five against two."

"Well, let's go then," I said.

"Okay!" Marvin said as he looked at Sammy.

"Sammy, you up to this?" Barry asked. "You know you can stay here till we get back."

"Yeah, but I'm locking the door," Marvin said. "You know you can't trust anyone these days. Someone might come in and steal our stuff. Get locked in here or go with us," Marvin said.

"I'll go," Sammy said, "and then I'll head home."

"Okay! Go it is," Marvin said. We all headed out the door, and then Marvin locked it. He put the key back in his pocket.

As we entered the alley, we were met by another pack of dogs. This time there were ten or more of them, some big and some smaller. Jake froze as he saw the dogs. They stood staring at us, but they turned and scattered at the sound of dogs barking in the distance, except for one, the one-eyed dog Jerry and I had seen earlier. He seemed to stand firm, as though he would not let us go by without a fight. He was big and mean looking, and looked like he wasn't eating well.

Then another loud bark came from a distance. Jake fell to one knee as the loud bark almost shook the area. Marvin looked scared too but had to keep up his image. As for Jerry and I, we looked at each other in the dim light and smiled. Jerry and I said nothing, but I was sure we both knew that bark. And I was sure Marvin and Jake knew it too. The one-eyed dog turned slowly and walked off like he wanted us to follow him. Marvin grabbed Jake by his jacket, pulled him to his feet, and whispered something in his ear. Jake said nothing; he just shook his head yes as he got to his feet and watched as Marvin led the way.

We all walked on. Marvin said, "Kid, let me use that flashlight of yours. It's dark where we're going and we can move faster with light. I know you won't believe this, Paul, but I had one like this. And can you believe someone stole it? The nerve of some people." No one found him to be funny, and seemed not to want him to talk. But he was the big gang leader, so they just walked behind him. I didn't though. I walked right next to him, and just as fast. Now Jerry, on the other hand, fell back with Sammy and Barry. I knew we each still had a pipe in our belts, and if we were walking into a trap, Jerry would be the first to hurt someone.

We made our way over to the train yard, but to my surprise we went around to the rear of the yard and through a hole in the fence. I could see that this must be where all the junk train cars and engines went when they died. "This is it, boys," Marvin said, "my office and our clubhouse."

"Aren't you afraid you'll get caught out here and go to jail again?" I asked.

"No, kid, this is junk. No one cares about this junk, and no one ever comes out here." I started to sweat, even though it was cold out. I didn't like myself right now for having put Jerry and myself in this spot. There was no Black Dog coming to my rescue. We hadn't seen a dog of any kind for the last few blocks, and now we were really on our own out here. Maybe it was my imagination when I'd heard that bark. I thought it was Black Dog.

"What's wrong, Paul? It seems you have lost some of that tough-kid thing since we got out here to my office. Don't you want to be my buddy? You could join our gang—and Jerry too. Might as well come with us. You're both wanted by the cops now anyway." As he talked, he stopped at the end of an old passenger car. Then, after going up a few stairs, he opened a heavy steel door. This time it wasn't locked. Jerry stayed to the rear. As we walked through the door Marvin stopped to light a lantern that surprisingly brought the old car to life. This old train car had seen its better days many years ago. Some of the seats were still in the car, covered with old blankets. A table sat between them with old food on it. And you could smell the pee from an old bucket that sat by the door, which had been used for a toilet.

"Where is Black Dog?" I yelled as I turned to face Marvin.

"Wow!" he said. "You should watch your temper. You scare your friends when you yell."

Hank stepped forward quickly, and Jerry went for his weapon. Marvin stopped Hank, so Jerry backed off too. "Let's go find your brother dog."

We left Sammy and Barry sitting in the car. Marvin led the way out to another old train car, only this was a boxcar without wheels, just sitting on the ground. There were no doors. As we walked inside, Marvin led the way with my flashlight. We saw the cage Jake's dad built, but no Black Dog.

"You lied, Marvin!" I yelled.

"Well, no, not really, Paul. I think we can find this dog together. You see, we owe you and your friend for all the trouble we have, and we owe that dog for what he did too. We read the papers about this big black dog and we called the newspaper. There are people who will pay big money for him, and we plan to collect. And now that we have you and your buddy, you can tell us how to find him. And until you do, you guys get to stay with us out here."

"I haven't seen him. And if I knew where he was," I said, "why would we have come out here tonight?"

"Because you haven't seen him and thought we have," Marvin said, "but you know how to get him. And if you help us, we'll share the money with you. Those people don't want to hurt him. They want to make him a star, and they'll pay big money for that. You might become a star too."

"Well, I'm like you, Marvin. Remember that night in the alley, after you hit my mom's car with those rocks?"

"Yeah, kid, I do."

"You said you don't rat on your friends. Well, I don't either."

CHAPTER
22 The Cage

"WELL, I GUESS YOU want to make it hard on us all, so if that's the way it has to be, okay!" Marvin said. "Put them in the cage!" Marvin yelled. Marvin grabbed at me, but this time I was ready for him, I twisted out from under his arm and stepped back out of the boxcar.

Through the dim lights over the street, I saw Jake grab at Jerry. Jerry knew what was next too. He pulled the pipe out of his coat like the super cowboy pulled his gun out in a western movie and was ready. He caught Jake in the ribs with that pipe. He swung at Jake like he was the last batter of the game and needed a home run to win. Jake wasn't ready for Jerry to fight back. He fell to the ground with that one huge blow and started screaming more of his foul words.

While Marvin stared in disbelief at what had just happened to Jake, I slid my hand slowly around to my back and came out swinging. Marvin tried to stop my advance but missed my arm by a mile. My pipe was longer than Jerry's, so as Marvin stepped in to block me, he must have misjudged. I hit him in the left elbow with all I could give. This time I heard something pop. I was sure it was his bone. He started swearing and threatening to kill me at the top of his lungs as he went down to the ground on his knees, holding his arm. I had no time to recover. Hank, just a few feet away, was standing just outside the dim light that covered the area. I hadn't seen him coming. I had to admit though, when I saw Jerry hit Jake, I felt some of that pain too. Just the thought of being hit that hard with that pipe was enough, but the sound it made as it hit was worse. I almost lost what was in my stomach.

Hank jumped me. We tumbled down a little hill and landed in some dirty cold water, with me on the bottom. My pipe sailed through the air and went out of sight. Hank tried to punch me, but Jerry pulled him back and held him for a moment, until Barry pulled them apart. I saw Barry say something to Jerry as he held him around the throat. Then Jerry threw his pipe out in the field as far as he could. Marvin was now standing, holding his arm against his stomach, and still screaming at me that I broke his arm and that he was going to get that dog tonight and kill it right in front of me. And then he would take care of me. His voice sounded different than it ever had before. He talked like a man in the movies, not like a teenager. He wanted money, and I knew he would do anything to get it, rob a train yard, rob a TV store, and even take his chances with Black Dog.

Marvin, with maybe a broken arm; Jake, with maybe a broken rib or two; and Sammy, hurt badly from the fall, left Little Hank, the mean one, and Barry. Now I couldn't figure him out, but no matter what he was like, he was one of them, and he'd have to pay the price. Like my Grandpa had told me so many times, you are what you hang around with.

Hank and Marvin, as hurt as they were, headed me into that cold, dark boxcar and pushed me into the cage. I knew I should stiffen up, because I was expecting to get hit from the rear. But to my surprise only a big shove came. I hit the other side of the cage. I couldn't see a thing, so I thought I would ask a dumb question. "Hey, Marvin, are you done with my flashlight?" Jerry was just being pushed in and the cage door was closing and locking when I asked. Marvin said nothing, but I could hear him breathe very hard. I knew he was really mad.

"I'm glad to see you, Jerry, or should I say hear you, because I can't see a thing."

"Wait till they're gone and you will," he whispered. "I didn't give my light away like some people I know, and I can't believe they didn't find it on me."

"Hey, Jerry, you're dealing with the stooges here. What do you expect?"

"Here, have some light," Jerry said. "And if I get the chance, I'm going to use this light on Hank and Barry's head, and then I'm going home."

"Well, it's good to be happy for the last time in our lives," I said, "because these guys want Black Dog real bad, and I think they'd kill for him."

"Hey, Jerry, what did Barry say to you to make you through that pipe away?"

"He said if Marvin or Jake got a hold of that pipe, they'd beat us to death with it, so I made it fly."

"Good thinking," I said.

Our Escape

CHAPTER 23

As we sat in the cage in the dark, cold boxcar with Jerry holding his flashlight, I asked him what time it was. He clicked it on and looked at his watch. "Ten to twelve," he said.

"Let me have your light a minute. I want to see something." I made my way over to the corner of the cage and set the light on the floor. I grabbed hold of the end wall, and to my surprise lifted it right out of the cage floor. It was heavy.

"Wow!" Jerry said. "How did you think of that?"

"Well, I'm sure a dog couldn't do that, so why weld it? And besides, I remember Mary said it came apart to move it."

"Oh yeah!" Jerry said. "I forgot. Let's get out of here. I'll left it and you slide under. Then you hold it up so I can get out. I'll grab the light," Jerry said.

We hid outside behind one of the other boxcars. I didn't want to say it to Jerry, but if these guys had too much time to think about what to do, they might do something really stupid to us, only because there was no Black Dog and no money for them.

After sitting a few minutes, Jerry asked me, "What's next, Paul?"

""Well," I said, "I think we should get out of here and make it back to camp before we are missed, and tell this story in the morning to clear us of that TV store theft."

"Paul, that's a great idea. Let's get out of here now."

"Okay! Go!"

As we made our way to the hole in the fence, we heard voices coming from the club car. Actually, it was more like laughing and loud talking.

We were about twenty feet from the fence when we heard a loud scream come from the club car. We stopped and turned to look to our rear, wondering what it was. Then we heard Marvin's voice behind us. We both turned quickly to see Marvin, Hank, and Barry. Marvin quickly displayed a slingshot, and told us to run and give him a moving target. "Paul," Jerry said, "I told you they wouldn't come empty-handed."

"Pretty smart of you, Paul, to get out of that cage. How did you know to lift up the cage?"

"I just used my brain, something you wouldn't know much about," I said to Marvin.

"You sure don't know how to make friends, Paul," Marvin said.

"Oh, now I should try to talk nice so we can be friends? I think we're beyond that point, Marvin." My knees started to get weak and I started to sweat, even though my clothes were still wet and cold from that roll down the hill with Hank into the muddy water.

"Jerry, maybe you should run and I'll use you for a moving target," Marvin said. "And, Paul, you can watch."

"Yeah! And me and Barry can use the target practice too," Hank said. They both held up their slingshots.

"And look, kid, we have these nice rusty ball bearings." Marvin reached into his coat pocket and pulled out a handful of what looked like balls of rust. He put them back in his jacket pocket, all except one. He loaded that one into the cup of his slingshot, and even with his bad arm he lifted the slingshot a little to take aim at Jerry's head. Jerry ducked down fast, but Marvin laughed and moved his aim to one of the boxcars and let the ball bearing fly. The ball hit like a bullet and sounded like a small explosion. I couldn't see because it was dark where it hit, but I'm sure it put a large dent in that old boxcar. "Now one more time, Paul, where is that black mutt?" My heart fell to my stomach as Marvin reloaded, aimed at Jerry, and pulled back on the slingshot. I thought for sure he was going to hurt him bad and there was nothing I could do. My fear left me feeling numb, and it showed. All of them knew I was scared more now than ever. Marvin laughed, and said, "Hey, Jerry! The next one is for you, not some old train car, but I think we'll let you and your buddy dog boy here run. And if you can get out of the train yard, we'll let you go."

As he spoke, Hank and Barry aimed their slingshots. Jerry looked at me with big eyes but said nothing. As we stared at each other, I could tell he was scared too. I was so sure that a slingshot would destroy almost anything it hit, and if it hit a person, it might even kill.

Then a strange thing happened: we heard the sound of a small bell in the distance. I'm sure the bullies never noticed the sound. Then we heard a lot of dogs barking. As we all looked around, Barry dropped his slingshot on the ground and said, "I'm not in this, Paul." He reached into his pocket, took out the ball bearings he had stashed there, and dropped them on the ground. I could tell he wanted no more to do with dogs in his lifetime after hearing what had happened to Marvin and Jake.

Marvin yelled at Barry, "What do you mean you're not in this? You're in it or you will be my first victim." He pointed his slingshot at Barry.

I yelled, "Marvin! I don't know where Black Dog is, and even if you kill all of us, it won't get you the dog or any money."

He turned his slingshot toward me and said, "Then I'll do what I have to." As he spoke we all heard the sound of that bell again, only this time it was closer. Marvin hesitated as he looked around. This time I knew what it was. It was the bell on Lady's collar. Then, like a large white ghost, she came through the air, lighting up the area with a white haze and hitting Marvin in his head and shoulder. She snarled as she flew through the air like she was wrestling a large snake on one of Mr. Chapel's camping trips. Marvin went down hard as he fired, only now his aim from being hit by Lady was off. He hit Jake with that rusty ball baring in his right arm as Jake came running at me from behind.

I threw myself on the ground just as he started to jump on me. He missed me, and Jake fell to the ground like a sack of potatoes, screaming, "That dog is coming to get us again." Hank turned to aim at Jerry and fired, but Jerry had hit the ground and rolled out of the dim light and out of sight. Hank missed him. He reloaded and took aim at me on the ground. I had nowhere to go—a pile of junk train parts blocked my way—so I just covered my face and rolled myself into a ball. I closed my eyes and waited for the blow. But none came. Instead I heard the sound of barking dogs once again, only this time they were right next to me. Then I heard Marvin screaming.

Slowly I opened my eyes to find Marvin on the ground yelling, "Help me!" He yelled it over and over again. Lady had taken him down and left the other work for her friends. I could not believe my eyes. There were all kinds of dogs, big and small, tearing at Marvin's clothes and, I think, at his skin this time. Jake was trying to get to his feet, but he heard, as the rest of us did, the bark of all barks, the bark he remembered from the alley on that rainy night while he hid in that dumpster. It was the bark of Black Dog.

Hank must have thought he could escape. He dropped his slingshot and ran into the nearest boxcar. Then we heard the bark that could only come from Black Dog sound out once more. More dogs came from everywhere. There must have been ten dogs headed into the boxcar where Hank hid, and fifty more dogs standing outside the boxcar. A scream that sounded like someone in one of those terror movies, which I don't like, came from deep inside the car.

Jerry came running from out of the dark and stood so close to me that I had to move away. "I'm sorry, Paul, but I think right now this is the safest place to be."

"Well, I'm not so sure of that myself, but I hope so," I said. We both stood and watched what was going on in total amazement.

Somehow Jake was back on his feet. He tried to grab me around the neck with both hands, yelling, "Stop that mutt of yours before he kills me." Suddenly, from out of the dark, he was hit from behind by one of the big dogs. He fell forward against me, and Jerry, being behind me, caught me, but we all went down. The dog was going wild on Jake. Jake pulled himself into a ball and hid his face with his arms and screamed out every foul word he knew. I wasn't sure what to do to stop this attack, but I knew I had to stop that dog before it killed Jake. Jerry and I scrambled to our feet and moved away quickly to avoid being hurt ourselves from Jake's now waving hands, waving arms, and kicking feet.

To our surprise, a large white German shepherd stood staring at us with big dark eyes and a large black collar with that very familiar bell hanging from it. Suddenly I realized a lot of things. One of them was like Randolph said: there are a lot of things in this life we can't explain. Jerry yelled, "Look, Paul, that's Lady over there by Marvin." I said nothing. I just looked into Lady's eyes and thought, *Thank you for looking out for us, and thank all your friends.* She looked right into my eyes and barked twice. I looked back at Jake as the dog was tearing at him. He was screaming more loudly now than ever. I yelled at the dog to stop, not knowing if it would listen to me or not, but to my surprise it let go of Jake. But it stood with its front paws on Jake's back and was still growling and bearing its teeth.

As I spoke to the dog to come, it turned its head toward Jerry and me. We just stared. Then Jerry yelled, "Holy moly, Paul, that's that one-eyed dog that's been following us all night long."

"Yeah!" I said. "Looks like Black Dog is here after all, and now we know where those barks came from all night, and why. He sure has a lot of friends." After we came to our senses, I said, "We better see what happened to the others."

"Yeah, let's go, Paul. Jake seems like he's in good hands. Or should I say teeth?"

We found Marvin as we both had seen him in the alley, only this time he was naked. He was balled up and crying softly, but there were still four dogs standing right next to him and a few standing further away. Lady was watching over the whole thing, standing proud with her head up high, just like a queen, waiting for him to move.

We had to laugh at that, but also we had to feel sorry for him. As we took a closer look, we knew that the dogs that had gotten him this time were not as kind to him as Black Dog had been. He had teeth marks all over his body but was not bleeding much. Jerry and I looked at each other but said nothing. We both knew that meant rabies shots, ten of them in the belly. Then I said, "Jerry, you think he would have learned the first time." Jerry just shook his head.

A few minutes later, we found Barry huddled in a pile of junk that he'd been able to climb into, with three dogs sitting in wait for him to come out, and one small dog, very mean sounding, still digging at the spot that he'd crawled into. We were surprised to find Barry uninjured. I knew he was different from all the rest, and I think somehow the dogs knew that too—that's why he was spared. Now on the other hand, Little Hank was not a good guy.

"We need to find Hank, Jerry. I can't hear him, but I think he's in that boxcar over there. And from what I remember, he had ten dogs or so on his tail."

We made our way over to the boxcar as carefully as we could, not knowing if all these dogs knew we were friends. We got to the opening in the car and stopped. Slowly I peeked in to find Hank was gone and there were no dogs nearby. I said, "Jerry! He's gone."

Jerry looked in and said, "Are you sure this is the car he ran into?"

"Yes, Jerry."

Then we heard someone yell from the direction of the clubhouse. "That sounded like Hank," I said. We made our way over to the clubhouse. But before we got there, we heard it again.

"Is anyone out there?" Hank yelled, only this time we knew it was coming from the boxcar where the boys were keeping the cage. Outside the car there were five or six dogs, big and small, looking very mean. We had to get in and find out if Hank had been torn up or not. We didn't like these guys a whole lot, but we didn't want anyone to die either.

"Jerry, follow me, but whatever you do, don't make eye contact with any of these dogs. I'm not sure they won't hurt us. We need to get in there and see if Hank needs help."

"That isn't the easiest thing to do, Paul. They seem to look in our eyes, and they seem to be looking for dinner."

As we entered, Jerry said, "Wait, take this. I lost my flashlight when I rolled away so Hank couldn't hit me with that shot he took at me, but I found it before I came back to you." I took the light and went in first without saying a word. As I entered the car, I shined the light around, with Jerry right on my heels.

Three more dogs sat inside by the cage door. They never moved a muscle, as if they were expecting us. Then I shined the light into the cage.

"Where is he?" Jerry said.

"I'm up here," Hank said softly, almost in a whisper. I pointed the light up to the top of the cage. He was lying flat on top of the cage as if he thought he could hide from the dogs. "Please get those dogs out of here."

"I'm sorry, I can't do that right now," I said.

"Are you bleeding?" Jerry asked.

"A little, I think, but if it were up to those dogs down there, I'd be dead."

"No, I don't think so," I said. They only do what they have to do. How did you get from that boxcar you ran into over to this one?"

"The dogs chased me in there and then got behind me, so I ran out. And they chased me again. Then as I ran to the clubhouse to get away, some other dogs blocked my way, so my only open path was into here."

"I think they wanted you in here, not in the other one. Did they bite you?"

"Well, there were a lot of dogs after me!" he yelled. "Not just those three."

"The other dogs are outside waiting for you," Jerry said.

"I was okay until I tried to climb up here. I got a few bites in my rear, and they got my boots, my socks, and one leg of my pants."

"Do you know where the key is for this cage door?" I asked.

"Yeah, it's in the clubhouse. Marvin threw it on the table after locking you in the cage."

"Well, I think the best thing for you, Hank, is to stay right where you are till we get back. And don't be fooled by these dogs being so calm. Right now their job is only to keep you here. Unless you want bigger bites in your butt and on other parts of your body, you won't move off that cage."

"They won't go wild again and come up here and get me, will they?"

"I wish I knew, Hank. But I do know this: you're better off up there than you would be down here." Jerry looked at me with a smirk on his face and just nodded his head yes over and over again.

We walked out a little faster than when we had come in. By this time we were sure none of these dogs were here to harm us. "Well, now that we know Marvin, Jake, Barry, and Hank are in good hands, we're going to look in on Sammy," I said. "He may need medical attention from that fall."

"Paul, do you think the dogs wanted Hank to move over to the boxcar with the cage?"

"Well, there was some reason they didn't get him in the first boxcar, Jerry, and some reason they wouldn't let him get to the club car, so yes! Somehow they knew what they were doing." It was just like when Black Dog herded Jake into the dumpster for Chinese dinner.

We went in the clubhouse to find Sammy was gone. Jerry grabbed the key to the cage off the table by the door. I said, "Let's go find Sammy." I turned to leave and heard a crash, and then I heard Jerry yell something I'd never heard him say before. It sounded like he'd taken speech lessons from Jake. I turned to find him trying to get back on his feet. I started to help him up by putting out my hand, but I pulled it back a little and yelled, "What's that smell?"

"I tripped as I turned to leave and fell on that pee bucket and it tipped over." I pulled my hand back all the way this time.

"Wait, I'll help you," I said as I looked around the lighted clubhouse for a glove or something.

Jerry said, "I'm up now, no thanks to you, pal." He was soaked with old urine and whatever else that might have gone into that bucket.

"Are you all right?"

"Yeah! Just sick to my stomach from the thought of what's in that can, and the smell sure could be a factor too, Paul."

I didn't want to laugh, but I couldn't hold it back. I let loose as I said, "Come on. Maybe there's a little water out here somewhere."

"Sorry, Paul, but a little water won't help. I need to jump in the Lincoln Park lagoon with all my clothes on." That just made me laugh that much harder. Jerry said, "That wasn't meant to be funny, Paul."

Again I said nothing. I just worked harder on holding back my laughter, but as I did a thought came to me: *I don't have to look back to see if Jerry is behind me now. I can smell him.* Then I started to laugh again.

Jerry just leaped on me from behind, where he was following pretty close to me, and said, "Okay, Paul, now you smell the same way I do. How funny is that?" We almost went down, but I was able to shake him off me. Still the smell stayed. Sammy was nowhere to be found.

CHAPTER 24

Roundup Time

"What time is it, Jerry?"

"It's ten to three, Paul. Can we get out of here now?"

"Sure, Jerry, but first we have to deal with the boys."

"What's left to do with them?"

"Well, let's go see if Marvin's enjoying all his new friends."

"What about Sammy, Paul?"

"Well, he was hurt pretty bad from what I could tell. I think he must have headed out and gone home before the dogs got here; otherwise, we would have heard from him out here too."

"Yeah! You're probably right, Paul. I think that scream we heard coming from the club car was Sammy trying to get up and out of here and go home."

"I think we should talk the boys into getting into the cage so they'll be safe from the dogs until we can get them some help."

"Yeah, like they're going to listen to us."

"Maybe not, Jerry, but I still see a lot of dogs around here. It won't be hard to convince them it's the safest place."

We checked in on Hank, and he started crying when he saw us, begging us for help so he could get off the cage and go home. "Okay, Hank, but when you come down, you have to get in the cage to stay safe from the dogs. Then we'll get the rest of the boys and get you help and a ride."

"Okay! Okay!" Hank said. "I'll do whatever it takes."

"Oh, by the way, Hank, what happened to Sammy?" I asked.

"Jake got tired of hearing him complaining and pushed him down the clubhouse stairs and told him to go home. Marvin and Jake just laughed as Sammy screamed going down the stairs. I knew he was really hurt," Hank said. "I think he started walking home by himself."

"Okay, cage time, Hank."

"You sure they won't get me?"

"Like I tell everyone, I'm not sure of anything, but we have to see. Slow and easy and into the cage."

Jerry unlocked the cage as Hank slid down. When he was halfway down, the dogs on the inside jumped to all fours and started to growl. That brought the rest of the dogs just outside the door to their feet. I yelled, "Okay, guys." They stopped growling but stood in place. I could tell they were hoping Hank would run. And I could see signs in their eyes that read, Lunch on the Run. Hank waited for me to say the next word. He slid down slow and stayed close to the cage. He slid in fast once he hit the opening, and pulled the gate closed behind him. Jerry pushed in the handle and started to lock it. "No, that's okay. I don't think he wants to get out without us around."

"Good," Jerry said. "Let's get the rest of them and go home."

"We need some of those blankets we saw on the seats in the clubhouse, for Marvin and the boys," I said. "I'm sure they're getting cold."

Jerry said, "I'm freezing and I have all my clothes on.

"Let's go," he said.

"See you soon, Hank."

"Hey Paul! What's that smell? Did someone die?" Hank asked.

Jerry turned and yelled to the dogs to get in the cage as he grabbed the gate. He looked really mad. I was sure Jerry was joking, but Hank ran to the back of the cage screaming, as the dogs started barking and biting at the cage. I called them off and they settled down. Jerry and I left laughing.

We made our way over to the clubhouse, but Jerry wouldn't go in. He said, "I smell bad enough, Paul. You go get them." I went in and grabbed the blankets, making sure I didn't step in that mess, and then I headed over to Barry.

We freed him from his pile of junk after reassuring him that he wouldn't be the next meal for all those wild dogs, as he called them. "As long as you don't try to run, and you stay with us," I said.

"I will, I promise," he said.

Now it was different for Marvin. He needed help getting up, so we had Barry help him. Lady sat firm, twenty feet away. Her bell never made a sound, I wondered what her part was in all this, and also I wondered if Mr. Chapel knew she was missing and if he was looking for her.

The other dogs moved back as Jerry and I came closer to Marvin. Then we had Barry come up. Marvin was talking loudly about getting all the dogs further away before he would move. I said, "They're not going anywhere, but you are, so get up. They won't hurt you with us around. But you need to put this blanket on you before you freeze to death right here in this junkyard that you like so much.

"We came back here to help you. Why I'm not sure. All you ever did was try to hurt us. But I hope that's in the past and that we can get you out of here before you die from the cold or those dog bites you have."

"Okay," Marvin said.

"Stand, but don't get violent or try to run," I said. "There's no Black Dog to take you down, but there are about a hundred other dogs around, and maybe more, that will. I'm not really sure, because you've kept Jerry and me a little busy, as you know." The blanket covered him pretty well, but he really needed a bigger one.

"Now off to see Jake and his guards," I said. As we got to Jake, we could see he was as still as he could be, so still and quiet that anyone else would have thought he was dead, until he heard our voices. He started to roll over and started yelling really bad words again. The one-eyed dog was his perfect guard and must have been appointed specially for him by Black Dog. One Eye grabbed Jake by one leg, turned him back onto his stomach, and went back to standing on Jake's back.

"Jake must have tried to get away while you and I were away, Jerry said. "He seems to have lost more of his clothes. And is that more teeth marks I see on him?"

"Yeah, Jerry, and I'm sorry to say that he'll need all those rabies shots. That's one every day for ten days, Jerry."

"Yeah, Paul! I'm glad it's him and not me." We could hear Jake moaning at our every word, from under One Eye, who had just lain down across Jake's body like a tiger hiding its dinner. "Well, time to go, Paul," Jerry said. "Can I have the pleasure?"

"Sure, Jerry, this one is yours."

"Jake, I'm calling the dog off," Jerry said, "but you know the rules. If you try to run, that would be bad for you but good for the dogs. And if you get tough, it will be about the same."

"Just call him off. I'll do anything you say."

"Back, boy!" Jerry yelled. One Eye stood up with all four paws on Jake's back like he was trying to get the last bit of fun out of scaring Jake to death. But Jake stiffened up like a board and took it the best he could so as not to get this dog madder in any way. Jerry and I laughed out loud at the same time, but Marvin and Barry stood quietly. Jake stood up slowly to see One Eye staring at him, looking as mean as the wild dog that he was. His tail was curled under and his teeth were long and sharp. He wasn't as big as Black Dog, but you could tell he sure knew how to take care of himself. And having only one eye made him look scarier.

I told them all to move over to the cage and not to talk or else they might scare the dogs and get them upset. They did just that.

As we walked to the cage with Marvin in nothing but a blanket and only one arm working to hold it, he lost it. There he was, bare butt and all. He stopped walking and reached down for the blanket, and the dogs went wild again, Marvin fell to one knee and let out a scream as though he was waiting for the attack. His eyes were closed tight and his arms were pulled up around his head, but Jerry and I yelled out "Stop!" at the same time, only this time my hand went up in the air. The dogs stopped and backed off. Jerry looked up at my hand, still in the air, and stared for a few seconds. Then he smiled and turned away. I knew just what he was thinking: *Like mother, like son.*

Barry reached down, picked up the blanket, and threw it over Marvin's back. He helped him wrapped it around his body like I sometimes helped my Grandma with her coat. Then Barry asked Jake for his belt. Jake was still in a daze. Still walking, he unbuckled his belt with his good arm from what was left of his dirty blue jeans and pulled the big black belt from the loops that held it. He handed it to Barry as if he were in another world. Well! I thought about that. What world would I be in if I had been hit in the ribs with a heavy peace of pipe, gotten hit by a rusty steel ball in my shoulder with a very powerful slingshot, and been attacked by a bunch of man-eating dogs that just tossed me around like a rag doll and tore most of my clothes off all in one night? One thing I did know: I was glad I wasn't him.

At the cage we put Marvin and Jake in with Hank and shut the door. "I'm not locking it because, like I told Hank when I put him in here, you'll have to get past the dogs to leave, so don't open the gate." I told Barry he had to come with us, call for help for his friends, and bring the helpers back here. I also told him to look for Sammy, saying he may need help. "Don't try to leave here until the cops come, though, because the dogs will only leave when they see the police. There will be a lot of them out here waiting for dinner, by the way. You three guys will have to go right to the hospital and start treatment for rabies. These wild dogs were not as careful as Black Dog was. You all have bite marks on you that drew blood. And from what I hear, rabies is a painful way to die.

"Oh, Marvin, I think you should get together with all these guys and think up a good story, but make sure you leave Jerry and me out of it and Black Dog too! You know, like when you came to my house and threw the lamp across the kitchen. You may not want our story told, and after tonight Jerry and I might not remember much about what happened out here, unless of course they come to us and ask.

"Oh, Jake, thank your dad for the cage!" I said.

"Hey, Paul!" Marvin said. "I have one question for you, if you don't mind."

"What's that, Marvin?"

"How in the world do you get these dogs to do what they do for you?" He was like another person, a gentleman with a sincere question, not Marvin the bully.

"Well, Marvin, I truly wish I could answer that," I said politely. "I can only tell you this. One of my very good friends told me that there are so many things in this world that can't be explained. But maybe you hit the nail on the head when you gave me the nickname Dog Boy." Marvin just shook his head.

Jerry and I headed out with Barry following close behind, but we were not alone. Lady followed close behind Jerry, and my newfound friend, One Eye, walked close to my left side. There were several other dogs, big and small, to our rear and off to our sides. I asked Jerry, "What do you think would happen if someone were to jump out and try to scare us just for fun right about now?"

Jerry looked at me with eyes wide open, and said, "Paul, I hope that doesn't happen. I've had just about enough 'fun' for a long time."

"Yeah! You're right, Jerry."

We headed over to the el tracks and down to Webster Avenue. As we got closer to Webster, One Eye stopped and started to growl. He was staring across Webster at the pizza place. At first Jerry and I couldn't see anything, and then Jerry said, "Paul! Move over here and you'll see what he must have smelled." Then Lady started to move to her right with her tail between her legs as two men walking down Webster got to close to us. Jerry stopped her as she started to lunge at them. Then I looked back across the street to see Sammy down on his knees, under the el in the dark. Barry stood very still as Jerry and I talked. "We need to help him," Jerry said, "and then get back to the park. I'm sure everyone and their brothers are looking for us right now, and I don't even want to think about how much trouble we're in."

I just nodded. Then I said, "Okay, let's go." The dogs seemed to disappear as we crossed the street, but One Eye and Lady stayed behind. They stayed right at our sides as we crossed the street and made our way over to Sammy. He was shaking bad and got sick to his stomach. He said he was trying to get home but couldn't make it on his own and thought that if he rested awhile, he could get there.

"That's why we have Barry with us," I said. "We hoped we'd find you so he can help you home. Or would you rather go to the hospital?"

"No, I want to go home."

"What time is it, Jerry?"

"It's four forty, Paul, and we need to go."

"Yeah, I know. Barry, help him home, but don't tell anyone about this night. Just tell his parents he fell somewhere. But make sure they know how bad he's hurt, in case he needs a doctor." We helped Sammy up slowly, but the pain was so bad that Barry almost had to carry him.

As we started to walk away, Sammy stopped Barry and turned his head to Jerry and me. "You guys, why were you trying to find me and help me, after we spent the last year trying to make your life so miserable?"

"Well, Sammy, I guess I get more out of helping than hurting. And besides, I was out here tonight looking for my friend Black Dog. I sure am glad Black Dog liked me and I was on his good side, instead of the other way around."

"Well, I sure am hurting right now, but I'm glad I got hurt before I ran into him again," Sammy said. "I might be in worse shape. And those two dogs there with you don't look too friendly either."

Barry said, "We have to go." As he turned, he saw see twenty dogs spread out around them. "Those dogs standing under the el there don't look too friendly either. Are we going to be okay?"

"I think they're waiting for us," I said. Barry shook his head and turned to help Sammy home. "And by the way, Barry, don't forget to make a phone call to the cops to go get your buddies."

He just yelled "okay!" as he disappeared under the el.

"We better get going, Paul," Jerry said.

"I'm following you, Jerry."

CHAPTER 25

My New Friend and My New Life

WELL, IT DIDN'T TAKE us long to get back to the park. We held our breath as we got closer to Mr. Chapel's tent. I was cold, tired, stinky, and still wet, and scared to death about what I would find at camp. Lady must have sensed no one was around. She broke into a fast run, and it was like we knew to run too. She went to the right of Mr. Chapel's tent, but I grabbed Jerry by his arm and said, "Not that way, Jerry. Let's go around the camp to the rear of the tent. As small as that bell is, it still might wake the whole camp."

"Go, Paul!"

"Jerry! I think she's creating a diversion anyway so we can get to the tent while anyone out here will be watching her."

"I should have known you were reading her mind," Jerry said as we broke into a run, with One Eye right on our heels.

As we both reached for the zipper on the tent, we heard a voice from behind us, which made Jerry and me both shiver. It was a voice that we had heard once before. We looked up to find one of those Chicago mounted police whom we'd hidden from on our way to find Black Dog. We heard him only once, talking to the other rider, but we sure remembered that voice. As we stared up at this giant on his horse, we were expecting the worst. I think we both stopped breathing. "Where are you boys going at five thirty in the morning?"

"Going?" I said. I looked at Jerry to help me out here.

"Oh! Well, we couldn't sleep anymore," Jerry said, "so we thought we'd watch the sun come up, and then go fishing when the chaperone gets up."

"Well, you're too young to be around the water this early. So get back in the tent and wait for the chaperone to wake up."

"Yes, sir," I said. "And thank you. We didn't know it was so early."

"Okay, boys. I don't want to see you out here alone again. Chicago is no place for kids at night. You could get hurt."

You're telling us, sir, I said to myself. "I just heard from one of our police officers that some boys were found in a cage over in the train yard tonight who might have been attacked by some wild dogs. So remember, strange things can happen." I snapped my head toward Jerry so fast that I thought it would take a week to go back in place. "Oh, by the way, boys."

"Yes sir?" Jerry said.

"Is that your dog lying over there?" We both looked where he was pointing.

"Yes, sir, it is," Jerry said."

"He needs to be on a leash and needs his collar on with his rabies tag."

"Yes sir, we'll put it on."

"Well, till you do, please keep him in the tent, so the dog catchers don't get him."

"Yes, sir, we will. And thanks." He rode off. Jerry and I looked at each other and smiled. We unzipped the tent and crawled in, Jerry first with flashlight in hand. Then I turned to look out at One Eye, who was now standing where he'd been lying a moment ago, staring at me with a sad face. And I have to say, we were reading each other's minds. He was asking if he was welcome, and I was asking him if he wanted to stay. I barely lifted my hand for him to come and he was at the tent door. He was in before I knew it, and almost knocked Jerry out the other end of the tent as Jerry unzipped the lower part to see if Lady was out there.

She had settled down right where she was when we'd left. I think she was as tired as we were, and almost as dirty and stinky.

When Jerry got his breath back, he said, "I'm going to sleep. And as tired and smelly as I am, please do not wake me for breakfast." His bed was still made up to look like someone was sleeping in it, but he could care less as he gave the pile a shove to the side and lay down next to it. I soon followed, clearing my bed first and then settling in, hopefully for a few hours of sleep. One Eye curled up at my feet, and we all slept like a rock.

CHAPTER

26 A New One Eye

WE SLEPT THROUGH BREAKFAST, and at about ten fifteen, Mr. Chapel unzipped the tent and asked us if we were still alive. I answered with a quick "Yes, sir." Then he looked inside. He got down on his knees and stuck his head further into the tent.

"What in the world is that smell in here, boys? And what is that thing staring up at me?"

Oh boy, I knew we were in big trouble now after all we'd been told about wild dogs and rabies. "I found him this morning outside playing with Lady when I went out to use the bathroom, so I sat down outside for a few minutes after I came back and he was really friendly, so I let him in the tent so the dog catchers wouldn't get him. My mom and dad said I could have a dog if I found one."

Jerry started to laugh. "I think you might say he found you, Paul." Then he laughed harder.

"Well, I think he needs me to look at that eye, Paul," Mr. Chapel said. "Get dressed and see me when you're ready. Did you give him a name yet?"

"Well, sir, I call him One Eye."

He looked at Jerry and smiled. "Okay, One Eye, Mr. Chapel said to come with me." One Eye didn't move. He lay at the end of my bed with his head held high.

"Go, One Eye," I said. "It's okay, he's our friend."

Then Lady stuck her head in around Mr. Chapel with her bell ringing, whined a little dog talk, and backed out of the tent. One Eye was up and out as Mr. Chapel quickly pulled himself to one side to get out of his way. "Those two seem to be good friends already," he said with a smile.

"Yeah!" Jerry said. "It seems like they have known each other a lot longer." I just looked at Jerry with stern eyes as he laughed out loud again.

It was quiet in the campsite, and that was good. Jerry and I needed that after yesterday, or should I say last night.

"Well, welcome to the world," Mr. Chapel said as we walked toward him. "One thing I know for sure, boys: there are four of you who need baths, and Lady is one of you. I don't know what One Eye was into, but I think it rubbed off on all of you. So I think you two should get clean clothes and make your way over to the bathhouse while Jeff and a few of the other boys give those dogs there a bath."

By the time we finished, the other boys had the dogs done and had most of the camp broken down and ready to pack into the truck. Jerry and I took down our tent and put it in the truck. Mr. Chapel called us over to give us some good news.

"I think you'll have to find another name for One Eye there. It seems he has an infection in that bad eye, but I was able to clean it out and get his eye opened. He'll need a vet to look at it, but I'm betting it'll be fine. And as for his limp, I found and was able to remove a small piece of what I think was metal. The paw was infected and tender, so I cleaned it out the best I could. That's another thing to have the doctor look at. A few of the boys are brushing him down. I don't think you'll recognize him."

As he spoke, we heard someone behind us say, "All done!" Jerry and I turned to see One Eye wagging his tail as I'm sure he'd never wagged it before. Jerry's mouth dropped and my eyes opened wide. We found ourselves staring at a different dog. He was as white as lady, and his eye was opened wide. He still had a slight limp, but Mr. Chapel said it would be gone in a few days. He also said that some good food would help hide those ribs. Jerry and I thought all that time he'd spent with us last night that he was gray or even light brown.

One Eye ran to us as Mike little released him. He smelled great and was wearing a brand-new black collar. "That collar is a present from Jeff and me," Mr. Chapel said, "for your new dog."

I thanked him more than once, while I hugged my new dog. "I know he needs a new name," I said to them, "but to me, he'll always be One Eye."

We packed up the rest of the things and headed out. This time one of the other boys got to ride shotgun, because Jeff and Lady rode outside with me and One Eye. Lady and One Eye stood with their paws up on the side of the truck. Jerry and I just looked at each other from opposite sides of the truck and never said a word. We didn't have to. We'd been best friends since we started school, but now we were brothers.

I couldn't help thinking about Black Dog and why he'd picked me to help, as he did with so many others. And I wondered if I would ever see him again. The thought was barely out of my mind when I heard One Eye bark as though he was crazy, and then Lady let out her own sound. I looked around but saw nothing. Then Jerry yelled out, "Paul, it's Black Dog, and he's not burned." I spun around from sitting flat on the floor of the truck and got to my knees as I heard the bark of all barks. This time I didn't cover my ears. There he was as we moved toward the corner, standing big and proud as though he wanted the whole world to see him, with his tail curled up over his back and his head held high. Next to him stood the old Oriental man with that long gray beard and that long walking stick that I had heard in the distance so many times in the past. The boys stared silently as we passed them. Mr. Chapel slowed the truck to almost a stop as he looked in amazement at this great large black dog. Lady and One Eye were both still standing, but now they stood even prouder, as though they were passing the king of all dogs. Black Dog barked one more great bark as we passed him. Somehow, as in the past, I was sure I was reading his mind. I knew he was saying goodbye to me, and also I knew he was telling One Eye and me to take care of each other. Then we all saw the old man tap his long walking stick on the ground as we passed. We all turned to see them again, and as always, they were gone.

Mom and Dad were a little surprised to find that I had left the house to go camping and had come home with a dog. Mr. Chapel talked to them and gave them the name and number of Lady's vet, and then he reassured them that One Eye was a very good dog. Then he had to explain why we called him such a name. Jerry stood right next to me as Mr. Chapel spoke, but he said nothing. We were both still tired and things were still moving too fast. Mom thought One Eye was too big, but Dad said he has probably through growing. Mr. Chapel said he thought so too.

I wasted no time thanking Mom first, with a big hug, and then Dad. I sure didn't want to give Mom any more time to think about it. I was reminded that all work having to do with the dog was mine forever. One Eye was still limping a little and his eye was wet, but Dad said we'd make an appointment tomorrow and get him fixed up. While Mom and Mr. Chapel talked, my dad put one hand on Jerry's shoulder and the other on mine. He bent over and pulled us close to him. "You know, boys, this dog is still young. I'm no expert, but I'd say maybe eight, maybe nine months old. He's thin from being out on his own and not eating well. But I bet he makes it to at least eighty pounds or more as he starts eating regularly and gets older. But, boys, best we don't talk about it around Mom, if you know what I mean. And one other thing, Paul," Dad said. Jerry and I still said nothing as we looked at my dad. "Can we change his name? He looks more like a good German shepherd than something that has only one eye, which some call Cyclops. You know, like Duke or Prince?"

"Well, Mr. Collins," Jerry said, breaking in, "I think if you give Paul here a few days to talk to One Eye, I'm sure they'll come up with his real name."

At first my dad looked at Jerry as though he were crazy. Then after a few seconds of looking from One Eye to Jerry and then to me, he said, "You know something, Jerry, you might be right."

"Oh! By the way, Paul," my dad said, "Randolph called this morning and told us that he had a long meeting with his people again last night, but he was sorry to say they have no new answers for us. But when they heard this story he told them about you and the Black Dog thing, all of them agreed on one thing."

"What's that, Dad?" I asked as Jerry and I waited.

"They all agree that you should write a book."

Jerry and I looked at each other and both swallowed hard. Then we shook our heads, laughed, and said, "No way."

Oh! By the way, Black Dog made the papers again.

As a matter of fact, he made them often.

But that wasn't a surprise, because he is a hero, and that's what heroes do.

THE BIG BLACK DOG

Reader's Report

THE BIG BLACK DOG" is the story of Paul, a young man in fifth grade in a Chicago school that has become pray for the notorious school bullies. Marvin Sikes and four of his sidekicks are seventh graders that love to pick on the weak and the defenseless. Paul run's home a deferent way everyday after school to get away from the bullies.

One day Paul run's into a very strange looking animal he thought was a black bear in an alley. After a long while and a real scare session for Paul, he realized it was no bear, but the biggest black dog he had ever seen in his hole life, never to see that big black dog again.

That is until the bullies decide that Paul needs to be taught a lesson. Paul is terrified when he discovers the bullies plot to beat him to within an inch of his life.

He took a longer way home this time thinking they would never find him. But to his surprise there they were. He new now he was dead meat, As they cornered him and Marvin pick him off his feet and through him on the ground. Things went on and Paul new the end was near. Then The bullies stopped and were looking at something. They were Frozen, without a sound as they stared behind Paul who was now standing. As Paul turned he could see the most amazing sight he had ever seen in his life, The Big Black Dog. He didn't know why he was there but he sure was glad he was.

That's where this friendship started but that's not where it ended. This mysterious Big Black Dog becomes Paul's hero and a hero to many others.

END

NEXT

ADOPT—ADOPT-ADOPT

Bullies seem to run ramped in our schools today, and we try to do the best we can to protect our kids from this very troubling virus. Wouldn't it be grate if we all had a Big Black Dog or at least a good little dog to protect our family and our homes. You can spend thousands on expensive alarm systems and cameras, but think about a dog. They can hear ten times better then any human and let a burglar know that they have been noticed. After you chose your type of dog and bring it home, Big or Small somehow they know you care, and soon after you get them home they know what there job is, and they become the family protector. We have all seen this, at one time or another

So if you don't have your own trained lion or even a great big bear for your home protector and you don't want gun's around to blow your own foot off when its 3am and you think you heard something downstairs, Go to the shelter and check on a dog. You can bet your life that he or she will make a big deference in your family life. And if you pick an alert dog[a little noisy] when you go to the shelter and take him home you will now have an alert family. Then when you think you hear that sound just look at Bowzer still asleep on your bed, give him a pet to say thanks, and get a good nights sleep. He may only weight 20 pounds but he'll fight like a Big Black Dog for his family.

Thomas Elliston Smith

Please Adopt

Printed in the United States
By Bookmasters